Navrisham Kaur Grewal

Born in Ludhiana to Jat-Sikh parents, Navrisham Kaur Grewal grew up in different parts of the country, from Calcutta to Kandla Port and from New Delhi to Mumbai.

An engineer and an MBA by education, she is the founder of Metalmate Robotics Pvt. Ltd, a leading robotics company and ChangeBhai, an online social impact initiative. Navrisham is a trained paraglider and can be often spotted paragliding above the scenic Pavana Lake near Pune over the weekends. She currently lives in Pune with her husband, Barinder, and their two cats, Bibi and Hero.

This is her first book and she can be reached at navrisham@gmail.com.

The Mysterious Disappearance of Five Rivers

Stories of my people ...

Navrisham Kaur Grewal

ISBN : 9789350643426

Ist Edition : 2016 © Navrisham Kaur Grewal

THE MYSTERIOUS DISAPPEARANCE OF FIVE RIVERS

(Stories) by Navrisham Kaur Grewal

RAJPAL & SONS

1590, Madarsa Road, Kashmere Gate, Delhi-110006
Phone : 011-23869812, 23865483, 23867791
e-mail : sales@rajpalpublishing.com
www.rajpalpublishing.com
www.facebook.com/rajpalandsons

For my parents
who taught me everything
&
all the Sikhs
around the globe

Contents

The Recurring Dream   9

Under the Banyan Tree   25

The Gold Digger   41

Desi Hip Hop King   61

Wanted - An NRI Groom   76

A Murder in the Campus   99

The Miracle Maharaj   123

The Five Metre Burden   139

Blood in the Ballot Box   153

Son of a Cabbie   166

The Recurring Dream

Standing on the nineteenth floor of his posh corporate office on West Broadway Street in Vancouver, Canada, dressed in an immaculately tailored grey suit, Baljinder Dhillon's mind races back, yet again, to the brick-paved streets in his native village, Bagha Purana, in faraway Punjab. Yet again...

...Wearing a knee-length white kurta with torn and dirtied shorts, he is running, holding a red kite above his head, followed by a group of noisy kids. Boys in shabby kurtas and girls in floral-printed salwar kameez without dupatta, trying to catch up with him. Crossing the Gurudwara Muglu Patti on his right, he yells in excitement *'bole so nihal'*...the kids yell back, catching their breath *'sat sri akal'*. The chase continues. He runs into the paddy fields. Many kids give up while others continue the chase.

Knock... knock..."May I come in, sir?" says a voice in heavily accented English. Adrian peeps in from behind the tinted glass door. Baljinder Dhillon snaps out of his reverie and hurriedly collects himself. He is back into his real world, his world since the last thirty-three years. Westend Realty Inc. One of the biggest names in real estate business in Vancouver selling 'Happy homes for you'.

An expensive antique-wood furnished boardroom, a public-listed company, 2300 employees and counting, the city mayor in the inner friends circle, a socialite wife Dally aka Daljit, a twelve room villa with five acres of landscaped gardens, three great danes and two beagles, two *firangi*... well...almost *firangi* kids. Mr. Baljinder Dhillon, Managing Director. Bally now, Ballu then.

Ballu was forced to go to Canada as a seventeen year old by his mother, *Bebe,* who had given him the example of, "Totaa who is earning big bucks in *Amreeka* doing nothing but just sitting outside a public toilet collecting coins." "Billu in England who is living a comfortable life after marrying a fat freckle-faced English woman called Rose," and "Rimpy in *Canedaa* who does nothing but take care of her three kids after marrying a rich 110-kg NRI Harry aka Harmeet."

"But *Bebe,* I like it here. I promise to *Waheguru,* I will complete my matric with more than 35 per cent...no...no...40 per cent...hmm... ummm... 50 per cent marks and take care of both our buffaloes single handedly and...and..." Ballu would assert in a single breath.

"Shhhh...*Chup kar oye,* (keep quiet) I have had enough of this life now, bringing you up on my own after your drunkard *peyo* (father) Amli's death. Go there, slog for a couple of years initially, get Permanent Residency by hook or crook and then call me there. This is what everybody does. This is what you have to do. We will live like royals thereafter...ever after..." *Bebe* would then drift off, lost in her world...a world that was a product of her fertile imagination and the concocted stories that she heard from Totaa's father, Billu's sister and Rimpy's mother.

~

Eighteen years ago Rajinder Dhillon, aka Amli, had married *Bebe* when *Bebe's* family was told by the village middleman, Nai, that Amli was the most eligible bachelor in Bagha Purana with twenty *bighas* of land and a house. Nai had told *Bebe's* poor parents "*Arrey*...my heartiest congratulations...*badhaiyaann...badhaiyaann...* You two are going to smother me by feeding *laddoos* when you hear about the match I have found for your daughter! He is the most famous boy of Bagha Puraana. World famous in Bagha Purana, I say. I can bet my wife on it, if a single person in the village, be it a man, woman or a child, says he doesn't know him... *Kismet khul gayi tuhadi.*" (Destiny has smiled on you.) *Bebe's* parents couldn't believe their luck.

A week later, *Bebe* still couldn't believe her luck! The Dhillons were heavily under debt. Yes, they had twenty *bighas* of land, but that was many years ago. Certainly, Amli was the most recognized face in Bagha Purana as he was found lying face down every day outside the village liquor shop, some 200 meters from the gurudwara, at dusk, and then at dawn again. Every man, woman and child going to the gurudwara knew him. Every day, women would comment in disgust, "*Chi...Naam kharaab kar ditta aa isne poore pind da..tut-painaa Amli.*!@#$%!." (You have brought shame on the entire village.)

~

"Bebe...Can't I go after one year?" pleaded Ballu.

Bebe aimed a tight deafening slap on Ballu's cheek. "Yeah right! You are leaving exactly after a week with Kaaku. I have already spoken to his mother."

Kaaku, their next door neighbour's twenty-two year old son was an Amli-in-the-making. He was to get onto Sea Princess, a cargo vessel from Mundra port in the faraway state of Gujarat. Kaaku's cousin, Sonu, who worked at the port had suggested this plan to him. Kaaku had told his mother, who was so excited to know that her good-for-nothing-son was finally going abroad and that too without her spending a fortune on an air ticket. An Indian agent was sponsoring the travel and the same agent had promised to get him a job in Canada. Kaaku's mother shared the plan with *Bebe* and suggested, "This is a golden chance for you to send Ballu abroad. We are so lucky. Both brothers can go together now. I am so relieved that there is someone to go with my son! *Waheguru tera shukar aa.* (Thank God) *Rabaaaaaaa.*"

So there it was. Plan finalized. Kaaku and seventeen year old Ballu were going to Canada by sea.

~

Exactly a year after *Bebe's* marriage was the first day when the men, women and children of Bagha Purana did not see Amli on their way to the gurudwara. He had died the night before, after puking *desi daaru* (local hooch), some *moongi-masri di daal*, one *roti* and lots of blood. Ballu was just a month old then.

~

Overlooking the skyline of Vancouver, Ballu or rather, Bally, is standing at the window with Adrian behind him, holding a brown leather covered diary with 'Westend Realty Inc' inscribed in gold on the top-right corner, reminding him about his business appointments for the third time since morning. He has already missed two of them. Baljinder Dhillon apologizes and then starts nodding in agreement as Adrian reads out his schedule for the rest of the day.

Ballu could still vividly remember his ride on the bullock cart from his village to the bus stand. Both boys were dressed in similar white kurta-pyjamas, with the pyjamas ending a good nine to ten inches above their ankles. Kaaku was sitting next to him, at the back of the cart, his dangling legs swinging back and forth. *Bebe* and Kaaku's mother were sitting in the front talking, as usual, about how life was a living hell in the village and how good Canada would be. They passed Muglu Patti on the right and the talking point for the two women shifted from, 'Oh-the-good-life-abroad' to 'our-drunkard-useless-husbands'. They crossed the *tobaa*, the village pond, green in colour, partly because of the algae and partly because of the reflection of the surrounding trees. Ballu wondered if this was indeed going to be his last trip on a bullock cart. "Oye Kaaku. Why do I think we will never come back?" says Ballu. Kaaku slaps his back and says, "Have you gone mad? Of course we will. We will reach there in a week's time and start earning from that day itself...three dollars per hour. I have already spoken to Totaa's mother. We will save money for a year and come back!" Kaaku got a tight slap at the back of his head from his mother. "Shhh...how many times have I told you? Dare you say a word about coming back. I will remove your skin and feed it to the vultures. Fat-brained loser. Just like his useless father. Nobody is coming back to this rotten village."

"See...I told you we will not come back," whispered Ballu.

Kaaku replied, "I am telling you...we will."

Kaaku was right. And so was Ballu. Kaaku came back and Ballu did not.

The cart passed Bhagat Singh Chowk and *Bebe* again started narrating Bhagat Singh's story to Ballu, maybe for the hundredth time in the last one year. Well, almost.

"*Puttar*... Remember the story of Bhagat Singh? You must become like him. Remember how he..." started *Bebe*.

Bhagat Singh was an Indian freedom fighter and regarded as one of the most prominent revolutionaries of the Indian freedom movement. At the age of twenty-three, he was hanged for shooting a British police officer and for ever found his way into history books.

Every time *Bebe* told Ballu this story he would be confused as to why was *Bebe* so adamant in sending him to a foreign country when Bhagat Singh was the one who was so in love with this country and had died for it.

They reached the Kotakpura road just outside the village bus stand and alighted from the bullock cart. It was *Bebe's* smart idea to wait for a bus there instead of going inside the bus stand, as she believed that that most of the long distance buses did not even enter the stand and just drove past it along the main road outside it. She bragged about her frequent bus trips to the nearest towns, Moga and Faridkot. Well, three trips in her thirty-eight years of existence. According to *Bebe's* calculation, all of them would be in the bus in the next half an hour. But her experience failed her. After standing for two and a half hours in the hot sun, a dilapidated bus drove past and entered the bus stand raising a cloud of dust and all four of them were left wiping the dust off their faces, clothes and bags. Her experience failed her, yet again. As they frantically ran behind the bus, Kaaku stepped on cow dung and his slipper got stuck in it.

Kaaku's mother yelled in exasperation and showered him with the choicest of abuses in Punjabi "#*@%$!...*Nalayakk ..Gadhe-da-saala, Chappalan-da-yaar*...Hurry up, you idiot...Just leave that damn slipper."

Kaaku ran behind his mother, Ballu and his *Bebe*, who were running behind the bus, limping exaggeratedly like a maniac, with just one slipper on. As he entered the bus, the conductor slapped him hard and pushed him down the running bus, spitting and shouting in disgust "Sheeshhhhh....what a stink!..Bloody low-class moron. Getttt outtttttt offf myyyyyyy busssss." Kaaku was back again on the ground wailing loudly. Meanwhile, a big fight ensued inside the bus between Kaaku's mother and *Bebe* on one side and the bus conductor and all the passengers of the bus on the other side. As the team of two ladies yelled at the top of their voices about the unfair treatment being meted out to them, the bigger team led by the bus conductor had people shouting from all over the bus. "*Chi Chi*..Stinking boy. Push him out of the bus or he will make our journey hell...Push...Push..*dhakka maaroo.*" People in various positions and locations of the bus, some sitting, some standing, partially sitting and partially standing cramped inside the bus, some hanging from the iron bar behind the bus, some sitting on top of the bus and some hanging by the entrance and exit of the bus. Either everyone's sense of smell was working overtime or it was an undeclared 'Boredom Day', the day when people simply wanted to have fun by creating a ruckus at someone else's expense, an activity quite common in Punjab.

So, out went the members of the first team, down the bus, one after the other. *Bebe* was the first to go. Kaaku's mother a close second, followed by Ballu who didn't quite understand what exactly the fuss was all about.

Kaaku cried loudly for the next fifteen minutes but stopped immediately after a taut slap-cum-pull-cum-shove from his mother, "All because of you!..$%#*!..*Botte da putt.*" They waited for the next two hours, inside the bus stand this time, and there came another bus, tilting precariously on its right and far more dilapidated than the previous one, but the bus was in no mood to enter the bus stand this time around. The team, now completely worn out, started walking out of the bus stand, half-running, half-walking and half-limping. The team hopped onto the bus without any mishap, just praying that they reach the Ludhiana railway station on time.

The conductor looked kind. Kind, weak, frail and old. *Bebe* and the team, recalled the serpent-like face of the last bus conductor and suddenly felt comforted and safe. Coins were exchanged. Tickets were given. Everyone got seats. Kaaku and Ballu sat together in the second row while *Bebe* and Kaaku's mother managed to get seats in the last row of the bus.

A popular Punjabi song by the famous singer Fukra Singh played in the background.

> *"Oooooooo ooooooooo oooooooooooooo*
> *Oh my beautiful beloved tell me one thing*
> *Why did you do this to me?*
> *Why did you leave me?*
> *Just come to me once*
> *I don't ask anything else from you my love*
> *I am drowned in my own tears when I think*
> *Of the promises you made and broke them all"*

A lovey-dovey couple was sitting in the seat in front of Kaaku and Ballu. Kaaku got all excited, "Look...look...lovers!!" Ballu was busy looking out of the window. Lush green fields. Clear blue sky. Women in colourful clothes. Men in white kurta-pyjamas ploughing the fields. Children running and holding thin sticks, rolling along tubeless cycle tyres. Little girls sitting on swings hung on the trees. White domes of the village gurudwara visible amidst the green fields. A water body would appear after every five to ten minutes. Ponds. Lakes. Canals. Rivers.

Kaaku nudged Ballu again, "Look...look in front...See see...what they are doing...hee hee!" Ballu found nothing amusing and retorted, "What's the big deal? Huh..."

Ballu, completely engrossed in the view outside had a strange sinking feeling, a feeling that he had never experienced before. He had a sinking feeling in his heart as if his world was coming to an end while all around him he seemed to feel a strange calmness.

~

"Mr. Dhillon, it is just a minor case of postural hypotension. No big deal."

Dr. Jane Pelletier is a doctor in one of Vancouver's leading hospitals.

"Thanks, Doctor."

"A drop in blood pressure due to a change in body position when a person moves to a more vertical position, from sitting to standing or from lying down to sitting or standing. No big deal at all."

Deep inside Baljinder knew that no words could describe this sinking feeling he experienced all the time, alternating between heart-tugging happiness when he thought about his past, his land, his people and a soul-wrenching sadness when he thought of his present life in this adopted land.

~

Kaaku seemed fully occupied with the scene in front of him and unable to control his mounting excitement. The boy was now playing lovingly with the girl's dangling pink earrings, matching with her pink suit-salwar, as the girl turned a blushing pink. Kaaku's day was made. Meanwhile, the ladies on the back seat were busy discussing the other bus conductor and rueing the fact nobody respected women anymore in Punjab. Their topics ranged from life-abroad to bad buses, lack of money to monotonous housework, a new suit design to a neighbour's daughter's wedding. Time seemed to have stood still for Ballu as he continued staring out of the window, at the people around him, at the fields...

~

Ballu and Kaaku had thought that their mothers would cry when they boarded the train at Ludhiana station but instead they were both smiling like Cheshire cats. In fact, Kaaku was the one who wept but Ballu did not shed a single tear. He knew he was going to miss his mother and his village but he had to fulfil his mother's dream. He was all that she had. All her hopes were pinned on him. He hugged his mother tightly and said, "I will come back soon, *Bebe* and with lots and lots of money. Don't worry about anything... Ok?"

"Ok...my son, am sure you will..but don't forget to call me...ok?"

"Ok *Bebe.*"

The train journey from Ludhiana to Mundra port was uneventful. They were lucky to get a seat in the unreserved general compartment and slept peacefully throughout their two day journey.

They stayed overnight at Sonu's place, who had arranged for them to board the Sea Princess, the next day.

Kaaku fell sick after a few days and was sent back from the first port itself. Ballu did not miss him. In fact, he was rather relieved. Kaaku was such a burden. Dumb idiot.

Initially Ballu was morose but gradually he made friends with the other people on the ship. Most of them were Indians planning to illegally sneak into different countries. The ship anchored in several countries on their way to Montreal but they were not allowed to step out. The ship docked in Montreal after more than a month of travelling by sea.

A person whom everybody referred to as Gianni ji came to pick Ballu and ten other boys at the Montreal port. They were all employed by Gianni ji at his cloth factory located on the outskirts of Montreal. Ballu lived with four other boys in a single room. Gianni ji was a kind man and put him into a local school where he slowly picked up English and the local French language.

By the end of the second year Ballu was made the factory manager. But then Gianni ji left for India and his son took over the factory. Gianni ji's son was the complete opposite of his father and Ballu did not get along well with him and soon after he quit his job.

Ballu started off on his own with a cloth shop and slowly ventured into other petty businesses. Though he failed in some, he succeeded in most others. At the age of twenty-eight he opened a property business and struck gold. And there was no looking back after that.

~

Ballu received the news of *Bebe's* death eight months after she had died. She was on her way to catch a bus to Ramuwala village to attend the wedding of her cousin's daughter. She was knocked over by a speeding truck while crossing the main road connecting Moga and Faridkot.

Poor *Bebe* lay unconscious on the side of the road for an hour before somebody spotted her. She died on the way to the hospital.

~

Baljinder Dhilon had a strange, lonesome feeling as he entered his house. Dally was flipping though a family album while the dogs were lazing around by her feet. He couldn't miss a hint of wetness in her eyes as she looked at the childhood pictures of their sons, Jaswinder and Harinder. Or rather, Jason and Harry. The boys had rechristened themselves as they did not like the names their parents had given them. They now lived on their own occasionally calling their parents once in three or four months.

As one of the servants came to the door to collect Baljinder's overcoat, Dally noticed his arrival. Baljinder couldn't help but comment, "How many times have I told you to stop sulking over these idiots, just let them be."

"Hmmm...Can't help it. How was your day?" Dally spoke in a monotone voice edged with boredom.

"Day was ok...just like any other day."

"Why are you becoming like me Bally. Bored with life...you used to be so full of life, *haan?*"

"I don't know. I keep wondering why I am here anymore. I just keep on thinking about my village and my people."

"What people Bally? Don't you know how things have changed in all these years? Thirty years is a long long time *yaar.* You will be disappointed to see that place now. I have heard, it is a big mess. And by the way, from what I hear, Bagha Purana is not a village anymore. It's a bustling town now."

"Thirty-three years and three months.."

"Ya...I guess."

"I don't know. I just want to go back to my village, at least once."

"Your wish. Go if it makes you happy."

"Will you come with me?"

"Please *yaar* Bally...don't ask me. You know how I feel about that place."

"Ok. Ok. Fine. I won't force you."

"Where will you stay? Surely not at some relative's place?"

"No. No! Am not sure if I even have any relatives left. I am not in touch with anybody now, especially after I sold my land there. Most probably I will book a hotel in Ludhiana."

≈

"Can I get you something, Sir?" asked the pretty airhostess on board Air Canada flight AC-9352.

"Just get me an Aspirin. I am not feeling too well," replied Bally.

"Sure, Sir. Please give me a minute."

She came back with an Aspirin and a glass of warm water on a tray.

"Mr. Dhillon!"

It seemed that he had fallen asleep. She called out to him a few more times but he continued to sleep.

She switched off the overhead light and walked away, taking the tray with her.

≈

An hour later, the flight landed at New Delhi's Indira Gandhi International Airport. The passengers began to move out of the aircraft one by one; and soon, it was empty. Well, almost.

The airhostess smiled when she passed by the business class seat 3B. Mr. Dhillon was still asleep.

He must be really tired, she thought.

"Mr. Dhillon, we have landed in Delhi."

"Mr. Dhillon."

"Mr. Dhillon!"

"Mr. Dhillon!!"

She tapped his shoulder softly. He did not respond. She sensed something was wrong and ran towards the front of the cabin and alerted the flight purser.

The flight purser came running and shook him vigorously. Bally's head dropped down on his chest.

"Oh shit! He is dead, Anne. Call the ground manager. Fast!"

≈

Ballu is feeling really light today, as if somebody has lifted a heavy burden off his chest. He feels as if he is floating in the air.

He in his village Bagha Purana. It is exactly how he left it thirty three years ago. Dally was totally wrong. He is standing in front of his house. His mother is waiting for him at the door. He runs towards her and hugs her.

"I am back, *Bebe*...I am back...I told you I would come back."

Under the Banyan Tree

As old age nears
It rusts our old gears
As we move ahead
No more worries about the bread
Gone are the milestones
Giving way to the headstones
Before we face the final curtains
Our stories will keep flowing, it's certain...

Someone once rightly said, in youth the days are short and the years are long while in old age the years are short and the days are long. This holds true for those men in their sixties, called the 'village elders', who gather under the banyan tree every day to while away the time which hangs heavy on their hands. It is a common sight in most of the villages of Punjab. This is their daily *adda* (gathering spot) where they spend most of their day, a seating area, made of *fattis* or wooden planks, under the banyan tree.

Railon Khurd Village, circa 1995.

Bikkar Singh : Where is Charna today?

Ajaib Singh : God knows! Haven't seen that bugger since quite some time now.

Bikkar Singh : Hmmm...What's with the bloody sun?

Ajaib Singh : It's terrible! The heat this year is unbearable. I was telling my grandson today that...

(Gulbagh Singh enters)

Gulbagh Singh : *Sat Sri Akal...Sat Sri Akal*

Bikkar Singh : *Sat Sri Akal.* Come, have a seat.

Ajaib Singh : *Sat Sri Akal* Gulbaghaa.

Ajaib Singh : Ya, so I was saying...What was I saying?

Bikkar Singh : You have become old...Ajaibaaa...

Ajaib Singh (sarcastically) : Ya...unlike you who is becoming younger day by day...hah!

Bikkar Singh : See... you have started getting irritated about such small things. Your end is near...start counting your days now.

Ajaib Singh (sarcastically) : Ok...I will if that makes you happy.

Bikkar Singh : Ha! You were saying something about your grandson...

Ajaib Singh : Oh ya...I was telling my grandson today about the time when I was his age. I used to cycle all the way to Ludhiana, play a hockey match and cycle my way back to the village. I did not care about the sweltering heat or the distance...but nowadays kids don't want to work hard at all.

Gulbagh Singh : Yes. Yes. That's so true. All they want to do is hide under their mother's dupatta when they are young and under their wife's dupatta when they grow up.

Everybody laughs loudly.

Nacchhater Singh, Sujan Singh and Satnam Singh walk towards the banyan tree exchange greetings and sit down.

Sujan Singh : Did you hear the story about Charan Singh's daughter?

Everyone replies in the negative.

Sujan Singh : His daughter ran away with the barber's son!

Gulbagh Singh : What!!!! Who told you?

Sujan Singh : At four o'clock in the morning when Albel Singh from the neighbouring village went to his farms, he saw them holding hands and running.

Bikkar Singh : That barber has three sons. Which one was this?

Sujan Singh : The youngest one apparently.

Nacchhater Singh : Have you gone mad or what? That boy is a polio case, his left leg is deformed and he can't even walk properly...how can he run?

Sujan Singh : Nacchhateraa...they checked with the Ropar bus stand, they were seen changing a bus from there. It was definitely the same boy!

Bikkar Singh : Oh ho! What is happening in this world!

Sujan Singh : Charan Singh and his relatives are busy running around trying to find some clue.

Bikkar Singh : And what about the barber Nathulal?

Sujan Singh : He fled the village with his family. What else will he do with his son eloping with a higher caste *Jat* girl.

Ajaib Singh : That girl looked characterless anyway. I kept telling Charan Singh to marry her off but he wanted her to complete her B.A. Now see what she has done. Brought a bad name to the family and the village.

Gulbagh Singh : Its *Kalyug* my brothers. (Kalyug, short of Kali Yuga stands for the mythological "Age of Downfall" at the end of which the world will come to an end and a new order of a peaceful global society will be established.)

Sujan Singh : Hmmmmm...

Bikkar Singh : What happened, Satnam? You are very quiet today.

Satnam Singh (mumbling) : Nothing...Nothing...

Nacchhater Singh : Hahahaha...it seems he has finally had his teeth removed to get his dentures done. What's there to hide Satnamaa?

Everybody laughs.

Nacchhater Singh : You finally listened to your wife, huh? You slave!

Satnam Singh manages a shy smile.

Sujan Singh : What happened to your compensation, Gulbagh? Is it done?

Four years ago, Gulbagh was one of the passengers on a train which was attacked by Sikh militants. A group of Sikh separatists had hijacked a passenger train near Ludhiana firing indiscriminately at the passengers they believed to be Hindus. Gulbagh, who was to get off at the next station, was walking towards the exit door and was caught in the firing and one of the bullets hit his right hand.

Gulbagh Singh : No. I am still running from pillar to post to get my government compensation. No luck yet...hope I get it before I die.

Sujan Singh : Hmmmm...at least you survived that terrible event. What were you feeling when you saw those militants firing left, right and center?

Gulbagh had been asked this question repeatedly in the last four years.

Gulbagh Singh : What was there to feel or think brother! Before I could even think anything, the bloody bullet had hit me!

(Gulbagh Singh was lying. He could still clearly remember the scene that day as he walked into the ill-fated coach S6 of the train he was travelling in. The train halted around a few kilometres outside of Ludhiana railway station. This is a normal occurrence when a train does not get the green signal to enter the station or another train is coming from the opposite side and has to be diverted to another track.

The train was in fact forcibly stopped by the militants as a part of a systematic plan to target the passengers in that particular coach. As the train stopped, two militants carrying guns entered coach S6 and started firing at the passengers. Gulbagh could hear desperate cries of men, women and children. There was blood everywhere. He tried to turn and run away when a bullet hit his right hand. He fell upon on a dead man's body and pretended to be dead. The militants stopped firing after the noise subsided. They then jumped out of the train and disappeared into the fields. There were no other survivors in that coach.

Gulbagh Singh could not feel his hand. He tried to get up but couldn't. He slumped down against the toilet and waited for help to arrive.

Police arrived an hour later. Ambulances arrived some thirty minutes after that.)

Bikkar Singh : That was a terrible time in Punjab. I had given up hope that it would ever end.

(Bikkar was referring to the militancy era in Punjab that began in the late 1970s and lasted till the early 1990s. Militants, proclaiming themselves as 'protectors of Sikh faith' killed more than eleven thousand persons between 1981 and 1993. It is estimated that more than 61 per cent of the people who lost their lives were Sikhs.)

Gulbagh Singh : Leave that topic. Let us talk about something else.

Nacchhater Singh : Did you hear the news about the *Sarpanch's* grandson? (A *Sarpanch* is an elected head of a village level statutory institution of local self-government called the *Panchayat*).

Sujan Singh : Harjeet? He is studying in Delhi *na*?

Nacchhater Singh : Yes. Harjeet. My sister's granddaughter studies in the same college as him. She told me that Harjeet cut his hair last week!

Gulbagh Singh : What a pity! The *Sarpanch* has been openly condemning families whose children are cutting their hair. Now what face will he show to the village people in the next *Panchayat* meeting?

Sujan Singh : I just want to see his face in the next *Panchayat* meeting!

The men spend the next few hours reading newspapers and playing cards. This was a well set routine for them and they never seemed to get bored with it.

The overhead sun has begun its westward journey and it is well past afternoon. The sun is setting. Men are going out to the farms. A few women can be seen going to the gurudwara. Some children are playing *gilli danda* (tipcat) some *lukam chupi* (hide and seek) and some can be seen simply rolling a tubeless cycle tyre with a stick and running after it.

A man wearing a white knee-length kurta with white shorts passes by guiding his buffaloes towards the village pond known as *'toba'* in local parlance.

Nachchater Singh : Oh my God. There comes Darshan. He is now going to bore us to death with his buffalo stories.

Bikkar Singh : Oh yes! he is just obsessed with his animals.

Darshan Singh : *Sat Sri Akal* to everybody there.

All of them just nod their heads with a bored expression while Darshan Singh comes and sits next to Bikkar Singh.

Darshan Singh : You are not going to believe it. Rajjo, my old buffalo stopped giving milk last week. What will we do now?

Bikkar Singh : Hmmm...that's sad.

Darshan Singh : And Rani's calf is not responding to medicines since yesterday...and...

Fortunately for everybody, soon enough, one of Darshan Singh's buffaloes strayed into a nearby farm and he had to rush to get her back before the farm's owner noticed it.

Nacchhater Singh : Thank God! I just wanted him to spare us the details. He doesn't fail to amaze us with his buffalo stories...they just don't seem to end.

Sujan Singh : Oh Nacchhateraa, you at least spare us now for the love of God. Change the topic please.

To Sujan Singh's rescue, his ten year old twin great grandsons, Ruppi and Seera, who have had a disagreement with the other kids while playing hide and seek, come and sit in his lap. Ruppi looked like he had been crying his lungs out and Seera's hair was all messed up with his top knot undone and the *rumaal* missing. Sujan doesn't even dare ask what happened to avoid being subjected to more tears and long stories.

Bikkar Singh : Hey...hey...look there...those women are going for the *guddi phookna* thing!

Ruppi (wiping his tears) : Where are they taking those dolls, Bapuji?

Guddi phookna is a practice prevalent in Punjab where women go to the outskirts of their village and burn home-made dolls of cloth while pointing to the sky. While they burn the dolls, they cry and entreat "Please give us rain, O God."

Sujan Singh : Son, they will burn these dolls to appease the God to give rain to our village.

Seera : Will God give us rain then?

Sujan Singh : Well, let's see!

Ruppi : But why are those kids running after the women?

Sujan Singh : Oh! The women are carrying *gulgulas* to offer to God and which will then be eaten by them and the kids. So run before they eat all of them! (*gulgulas* are similar to mini doughnuts.)

Seera and Ruppi run off along with the other kids, yelling, "Rain will come...rain...rain...rain."

Gulbagh Singh : Ah! The joys of childhood!

As they get ready to begin another game of cards, they see Sukwant Kaur coming towards them. Sukhwant Kaur is around eighty years old but fit as a fiddle. All the men including Ajaib Singh are a little taken aback to see a woman approach their 'all-men spot' so audaciously. But then it's Sukhwant Kaur. She can do anything. Surprisingly, she is walking with a slight limp today. There has to be a story behind this limp.

Her sole purpose in life nowadays is to harass Ajaib Singh and his family into selling off a small ancestral land next to her house. She leaves no stone unturned to scare the women in his family and now, as he could guess, it was his turn.

Sukhwant Kaur : *Sat Sri Akal* Ajaib Singhaa.

Ajaib Singh : *Sat Sri Akal* Sukhwant Kaur.

Sukhwant Kaur : You are not going to believe what happened when I went out last night towards my buffalo shed to check on Rano, my old buffalo.

Ajaib Singh : What happened? Everything all right?

Sukhwant Kaur and Ajaib Singh are second cousins. Their grandfathers were brothers. Sukhwant Kaur never married. Somebody got saved!

Sukhwant Kaur : I was passing by your land yesterday at around ten o'clock when I heard someone say "Sukhwant Kurae...where are you going so late in the night?" I just looked back to locate this person. And you won't believe what I saw?

Ajaib Singh : What? Who?

Sukhwant Kaur : I..I...I.. saw a ghost sitting on top of the mango tree in your land..and before I could react..he came flying towards me and kicked me on my back.

Ajaib Singh : What nonsense!

Sukhwant Kaur : If you don't believe me, ask the village doctor who has just treated me. I have been warning your family for the last six months about strange things happening on your land...but you just don't seem to listen.

Ajaib Singh : Strange things. Like what?

Sukhwant Kaur : Like...like. These weird shaped figurines made of dough that somebody is throwing from your side into our house at all odd hours...and my brother's grandson has been sick since the day one of these hit him on the head. He has been vomitting strange things since that day.

Ajaib Singh : Take him to a doctor.

Sukhwant Kaur : Of course we took him to the *mandi* doctor. The doctor was surprised when he saw him puking chains, amulets, spider webs!

Ajaib Singh : Ok. Ok. Fine. You go from here now. We will talk about this later.

Sukhwant Kaur : Ok. Ok. I too have to go to the gurudwara now anyway.

Sukhwant Kaur leaves chanting *waheguru..waheguru..waheguru...*

Gulbagh Singh : What the hell is wrong with this woman?

Ajaib Singh : Nothing new for me. This has been going on for months now. She wants us to sell that small piece of land next to her house because she wants to tie her buffaloes on that land.

Sujan Singh : Then sell it. It's of no use anway, nothing grows on it because of the sand.

Ajaib Singh : I agree, but Sukhwant wants me to sell it off for peanuts.

Sujan Singh : My God!

Ajaib Singh : What else did you think? Is it fun listening to these weird ghost stories all the time! God! When will this woman give up?

Sujan Singh : Hmmmm...

A young man on a bullock passes by the banyan tree. His cart is full of cow-feed. He waves to the group and greets them enthusiastically.

Bikkar Singh : How is the crop this year Gurbakshaa?

The youngman's name is Gurbaksh Singh and he is in his mid-thirties. He had left the village fifteen years ago to join the Indian Army but came back within a year for reasons best known to him. Some villagers speculate that he was dismissed from the Army on disciplinary grounds while some say that he ran away as he could not handle the pressure. He is a farmer now.

Gurbaksh Singh : Bad...bad...hope it rains soon or we will have nothing to eat this year.

Bikkar Singh : Hmmm...Did you find a bride finally? I have heard some gossip of late.

Gurbaksh Singh : No...Not yet.

Bikkar Singh : Take my advice, son. Don't be so choosy now.. Time is slipping by.

Gurbaksh Singh : Yes. Yes. Of course.

Gurbaksh leaves as fast as he had come. He is used to such 'marriage related' advice and doesn't take it seriously anymore. Everybody has a comment to make on this topic.

Bikkar Singh : All these boys want to have a say in whom they will marry and they don't seem to appreciate our advice. Back in our days, the village barber used to fix marriages and we would see our bride's face only on the wedding night.

Ajaib Singh : So true...and remember the bride used to sit with a heavy quilt covering her face and one could never make out whether it was a boy or a girl or an animal. Ha! Ha! Ha!

Sujan Singh : Yes...yes...

Ajaib Singh : And...in every wedding...there would be a huge fight after a few drinks.

Sujan Singh : Oh...yes...there was always a fight.

Bikkar Singh : But...those were the days...

Gulbagh Singh (wiping away his tears) : And what else? Anybody planning to go to Hemkunt Sahib this year?

Hemkunt Sahib is a Sikh place of worship devoted to the tenth Sikh Guru, Guru Gobind Singhji. Located in the Himalayas at a height of around 15,000 ft. it is in the middle of a glacial lake surrounded by seven mountain peaks.

Ajaib Singh : At this age! No...no...

Sujan Singh : It is better to remember God from here only rather than climbing all the way. What about you?

Gulbagh Singh : I will go with my sons. It has been three years since I last went. I am a great believer in the power of that place.

Bikkar Singh : Hmm...Good..good...get some blessings for us as well.

The evening light is beginning to fade into darkness. Everybody is leaving. After the last person is out of sight, Bikkar Singh gets up and leaves for his house which is around twenty minutes walking distance from the *adda*. He unlocks the door of his house, goes to the kitchen, takes some wheat flour from a steel canister and starts kneading dough.

Since his only son left for Canada to find work, Bikkar Singh has been living alone. The boy has never called. Bikkar doesn't even know if he is still alive.

≈

Meanwhile, Seera and Ruppi are sitting in their front yard and waiting for the elusive drops of rain while their mother is trying to convince them to come inside.

≈

"Bloody idiot, what does he think? If he doesn't give me money, I won't be able to get my liquor bottle or what!" a middle-aged man is loitering around in the dark near the banyan tree where the elders spend their day. He is holding a local liquor bottle in his hand and appears completely drunk.

"Why is he still alive in the first place is something I do not understand? Why can't he just put the land in my name and die?"

"I am going to burn down this whole damn place..am sure he will die when he sees this...to hell with you ..father...to hell with you!" he says as he pours some liquor on the wooden bench under the banyan tree and throws a lit match stick on it.

≈

Next morning, the villagers are gathered at the place where till yesterday the banyan tree used to stand. The banyan tree has disappeared and all that is left of it is a barely two feet burnt stump of the trunk.

A little distance away, a middle aged man is lying face down. He seems unconscious with some burn injuries on his right hand. A few inquisitive teenagers come and turn him around to see his face.

"It is Sujan Singh's elder son Sukhwant Singh!" shouts a teenager with a fancy beard and ear studs.

"His hands are burnt!" says another boy with an equally appalling sense of fashion

"That's good news...he would not be able to pick up a liquor bottle again in his life...hah!" adds Sukhwant Kaur, matter-of-factly and with a menacing smile on her face.

All the men stand around quietly, not knowing what to do. Now where will they sit and how will they while away the long, lonely hours of their remaining days...

The Gold Digger

Delhi, circa 2009. "Ahluwalia Niwas" in Greater Kailash-I, more popularly known as GK-I in local 'Dilli' parlance. A family of four : Sahbaz Singh Ahluwalia, Davinder Kaur Ahluwalia aka Dolly, Gurkeerat Singh Ahluwalia aka Guri, age 19, and Loveleen Kaur Ahluwalia aka Baby, age 15

Sahbaz Singh Ahluwalia's grandfather, Gurdayal Singh Ahluwalia, had arrived in Delhi sixty-two years ago after an unprecedented forced migration that followed the partition of India in 1947. Gurdayal Singh Ahluwalia was part of a contingent of the thousands of Hindus and Sikhs from the North West Frontier Province, who fled to India's capital to make it their new home.

He was accompanied by his wife and ten year old son, Sukhcharan. They spent seven months in a refugee camp at the military barracks in Kingsway in Delhi, one of Northern India's largest refugee camps with more than thirty-five thousand refugees at any given time. Luckily, for this family of three, Gurdayal Singh was successful in receiving the one thousand rupee loan provided by the administration under a scheme for refugees to restart their business and life. From his teenage years, Gurdayal had assisted his father in his tailoring shop in Swari, one of the longest markets in the North West Frontier Province. This experience now came in very useful as he started a tailoring unit in a small shed on the outskirts of Delhi. Over the years the business prospered and by the time Sukhcharan turned twenty five, the Ahluwalia family lived comfortably and was regarded as one of most influential families of the area. Gurdayal Singh Ahluwalia purchased a large residential plot in the early 1960s when a new area called Greater Kailash was being developed and built a sprawling bungalow on it and named it 'Ahluwalia Niwas'.

Fortunately for the Ahluwalias, Sukhcharan inherited his father's enterprising temperament and displayed exceptional business acumen from a very young age. He had been assisting his father in the tailoring unit, which had grown from a small shed to several sprawling modern factories in and around Delhi and branched out into diverse businesses such as soft drinks, bakery and construction. After three daughters, Sukhcharan's wife Harminder gave birth to a baby boy, Sahbaaz Singh Ahluwalia.

Sahbaaz was an average student who managed to score decent marks in his school. Like other children born with a silver spoon, he too was sent abroad to study management after he completed his graduation from Delhi University. He was not very enterprising but just good enough to leverage his limited strengths and manage the business empire his father and grandfather had built.

≈

One evening Sahbaaz was returning home after watching a late night show of the movie *Love 86*. In the movie, two boys Vicky and Omi, fall in love with two sisters who had been instructed by their mother to find wealthy husbands for themselves. The girls end up falling in love with the two heroes, who actually were petty thieves.

After watching the movie, Sahbaaz vowed to himself that in the next ten days he too must fall in love, come what may. Driving his new imported white Mercedes E-class and listening to the songs of *Love 86*, Sahbaaz saw a popular *paan* stall still open in Kailash Colony market and decided to have a *paan*. He parked his car a little distance away and started walking towards it. At the same time, Dolly was taking an after dinner walk along with her younger sisters when she heard someone whistling the tune of her favourite song from *Love 86*. Dolly turned around to see who was whistling and she saw Sahbaaz. Both Dolly and Sahbaaz looked at each other and it was 'love at first sight'.

~

Unlike Sahbaaz's family, Dolly came from a modest, service class family. Her father, Harkishan Khurana, was a manager at the State Bank of Patiala. He had come to Delhi from Ludhiana in early 1965 after completing his graduation. He cleared the bank recruitment examination and landed a job as a junior level officer at SBP where he had been working diligently ever since. On a brief visit to his hometown Ludhiana, he was married off to Chandni Suri, now Mrs. Khurana. Exactly nine months after their wedding the Khuranas welcomed their first child, Davinder aka

Dolly. Two other girls, Ravinder and Surinder, were born soon after. Despite mounting pressure from relatives and freinds, the Khuranas decided not to have a fourth child in anticipation of a son, which is the most desirable outcome of every pregnancy in most Punjabi families.

As a teenager, Dolly hankered for all fancy, expensive things that she saw the 'high-class babes of GK' flaunt. She loved to hang out at GK-1 M-Block market with her sisters and friends though all she ever bought from there were some cheap beaded necklaces and accessories sold by roadside vendors. She would spend her Saturdays and Sundays hanging around in the market looking at and envying the 'GK babes'. Her only dream in life was to be one of them. She longed to dine at the classy restaurants and shop at outlets of luxury brands. She bought fake branded clothes that appeared as close to original as possible from the street markets of Sarojni Nagar, Palika Bazaar and Paharganj.

Dolly was a poor student and just about managed to clear her twelfth standard exams. She hated school and everything about it. Her sisters were good students which did not help her case at all. Her father often reprimanded her for her lack of interest in studies and excessive inclination towards fashion. But, for her it was simple. She would rather catch a train to Siberia than study. Dolly's father would often tell his wife to reason with her to get her back on track, but in vain. Not only did Dolly not listen to her mother but also had the audacity to try and convince her of the fact that women are made for all the good things in life and not to slog their asses off in doing household chores like her. Dolly's father finally gave up the day he noticed his wife's shapely eyebrows! Dolly had talked her simpleton mother into getting her eyebrows threaded at a neighbourhood beauty parlour.

Dolly's best friend was Eveneet Ahuja aka Pinky. Their mothers were from the same village in Punjab and the two girls had been inseparable from the time they were toddlers. While Pinky's world revolved around boys, Dolly was obsessed with clothes and lifestyle.

When Pinky and Dolly were not loitering about at their favourite shopping haunt they would while away their time discussing boys. Pinky had brought it to Dolly's notice that their class topper, Pratyaksh Singh, was interested in her and that she often caught him staring at her in the classroom.

Dolly kept an eye on him from the next day onwards and was convinced that Pinky's suspicion held some weight. She also got a confirmation from a common friend, Rajiv, who went to the same tuition class as Pratyaksh. Apparently, Pratyaksh had been in love with Dolly (for him, she was Davinder Kaur from Class 12, Section B) for the last five years. Secret love is a common occurrence in schools and colleges of North India where a boy picks a girl as his love interest and shares this information with all his friends. This is followed by his friends referring to the girl as their *bhabhiji* or sister-in-law. As an unwritten rule, no other boy can express interest in that particular girl. The girl has no inkling of this while the boy often gets into fights with others over 'breach of territory'. This breach can be either oral, where the other guy just declares his interest in that particular girl or physical wherein he goes and proposes to the girl in person. But the fact that the boy is interested in the girl is kept a top secret from the girl. This goes on for years until: the girl gets engaged or married; a pesky girlfriend tells the girl about it citing unnamed sources; the girl starts dating somebody else; or the boy gives up.

Pratyaksh was a good looking and well-mannered Sikh boy. Fair-complexioned, tall, intelligent. These were fairly important but secondary qualities that Dolly always wished her man should have, the primary one being 'rich'.

One day Dolly and Pinky got into an auto rickshaw and followed Pratyaksh home from his tuition class. They saw him enter a rather unassuming single storey tenement style house with a bottle green coloured Bajaj SuperNE scooter parked in the front yard. The house as well as the scooter seemed to scream 'lower middle class'. Pinky gave one rupee to the auto rickshaw driver to knock on the next door neighbour's house and ask for Mr. Singh's house. The driver did as he was told. A middle-aged woman opened the door. She was dressed in a nightgown with a dupatta, a typical dress worn by lower-middle class housewives in Delhi. She looked warily at the driver and asked, "What do you want?"

"Oh...mm...madam ji. Can you please tell me which one is Mr. Singh's house? I need to deliver a wedding card to them from the Roshans," blurted out the driver, the exact words the girls had instructed him to say.

"This is Delhi. There are a lot of Mr. Singhs here...Which one are you talking about?"

"They have one son, Pratakss and...and..." said the driver trying to recall the sister's name the girls had told him.

"Oh! Truck driver Singh sahib! Ya, he stays next door. He has a son Pratyaksh and a handicapped daughter Sonakshi. Same one *na*?" the woman asked cheerfully, happy to divulge additional information.

"Oh yes...same same...thank you ji," the driver replied before turning around and walking towards his auto rickshaw.

"*Arre* memsahib, some truck driver Singh stays in that house with his son Pratakss and daughter Sonaksi," the auto rickshaw driver told the girls making a funny hissing sound at the end of Pratyaksh's name, Prataksssss.

"Truck driver!" screamed Dolly and Pinky.

After this revelation, no words were exchanged between them and they just headed home. They got down and Dolly quietly handed over an extra ten rupees to the driver, over and above the rickshaw fare.

This was the end of the chapter for Pratyaksh and all discussions concerning him. This was duly conveyed to him by Rajiv. When Pratyaksh politely asked him the reason for the refusal, Rajiv coldly replied, "Dolly says that she is not interested in you because you are poor."

Pratyaksh was heartbroken. He had planned to propose to Dolly after getting admission into one of the IITs as he had cleared his IIT JEE exam with flying colours and had got an all India rank of 24. He had the option to select any branch of engineering in any of the IITs. He had decided he would go IIT Bombay, which had always been his dream. His tutor and mentor, Sudharshan

Govind, had told him that once he got into IIT his life would be made and there would be no dearth of girls who would want to marry him. Alas! Life is unfair and does not go as planned. He cursed himself for not proposing to Dolly the day he got his IIT JEE result. He had been so confident that she would agree but was he mistaken!

Little did he know that Dolly didn't believe in future prospects however brilliant they may be and the wealth that 'may' come. She wanted everything right then. The next day, Rajiv was sent to explain this to Pratyaksh in clear and concise words.

Rajiv met him in the school park. "Listen...Davinder wants to marry someone who stays in a place like GK and whose father is stinking rich...RICH is the keyword my poor friend," Rajiv said with a smirk on his face.

Pratyaksh got the message that it was all over and that he could never get Dolly.

As a sullen-faced Pratyaksh stood there, Dolly and Pinky watched from a distance peeping from behind a pillar. "What a waste of time *yaar* Pinky!" said Dolly. Pinky just nodded though she felt bad for the poor boy and was quite taken aback by Dolly's cold comment. Waste of time!

~

Sahbaaz and Dolly's eyes met briefly before her sister Rani nudged her. Sahbaaz kept staring at her as she moved ahead quickly with her sisters and entered a house. Sahbaaz continued standing there in the hope that Dolly would come out to have a look at him, just the way it happened in the movies. Five minutes. No luck. Ten minutes. Still no luck. Twenty two minutes. What the hell! Twenty two minutes. Oh! There she was, peeping from behind the curtains of a small window on the first floor. It is a YESSSSSSS!!!!!

Sahbaaz pumped his fist in the air, turned around and jauntily walked towards his car.

The next day, Sahbaaz, was back at the same spot where he had seen Dolly last night. He was accompanied by two of his closest friends, Vicky Ahuja and Rahul Mahajan, sons of a leading liquor business tycoon and a Lok Sabha MP respectively. According to GK inner gossip, Sukhcharan and Vicky's father had spoken about a marriage alliance between Sahbaaz and Vicky's sister Meghna. This was not known to Sahbaaz but Meghna had always been made to believe that she would get married to Sahbaaz at the right time. Meghna had been in love with Sahbaaz since childhood.

Sahbaaz had told Vicky and Rahul about 'this girl' that he had fallen in love with. They made fun of him and thought he was joking. Sahbaaz told them that she was the prettiest girl he had ever seen.

Meanwhile, Dolly, deep down in her heart, was expecting the tall, handsome and rich looking boy to return today. Restlessly she kept looking outside her window and when she had almost given up hope, there he was! Dressed in a white collared Tommy Hilfiger T-shirt and high-waist blue jeans, he was standing near the *paan* stall and looking up at her window. There were two more guys with him. They too looked rich.

Dolly's mother and father were home that day, so she made an excuse of going to Pinky's house for clearing some doubts about her maths homework. She quickly ironed her best dress, an ankle-length peach coloured frock with a white floral design. She also put on a white belt, a white hair band and white wedge-heel sandals. She had bought the dress from Lajpat Nagar and the accessories from Karol Bagh last month and had reserved them for a special occasion.

Sahbaaz saw her coming out of her house. She looked very pretty albeit a tad bit overdressed for a hot September evening. She was tall, fair skinned and petite. She had an innocent looking face with a mole above her lip. She looked a little like Rati Agnihotri, a Hindi film actress known for her innocent face and sexy image. He was so in love with her!

Vicky and Rahul smirked as they saw her. She was really pretty but looked like a typical gold digger to them. They were not impressed and were sure that their friend Sahbaaz would soon get over her.

~

Sahbaaz and Dolly dated for almost two years before getting married in August 1988. The theme for their wedding was 'royalty'. Palace themed rooftops, velvet curtains and chandeliers were used to give the wedding set-up a majestic look. The marriage was a grand affair with the who's-who of the city in attendance. They were all there - fashion pharaohs, high-flying honchos, liquor barons, powerful politician, pop stars and movie stars.

There were more than five thousand guests in attendance from across the globe. A popular film star performed at a specially created stage which was suspended in the air. Surprisingly, the person who appeared most awestruck with the whole set-up was the bride herself! Dolly had to repeatedly pinch herself to make sure that this was really happening. She had always known that she would hook herself a rich guy, but this was much more than what she had ever imagined.

Sahbaaz's grandfather was a happy man on the wedding day. He had risen from modest beginnings himself and hence had no pretensions whatsoever, as long as the girl was a Punjabi. Sukcharan, Sahbaaz's father, was initially against the match but had to agree because of pressure from his father as well as his son. Sukhcharan wanted his son to marry Meghna Ahuja, who was not only beautiful but came from a reputed family. Meghna was handling her father's poultry and cosmetic business successfully and was an engineer from the prestigious Delhi College of Engineering and hence, an appropriate match for Sahbaaz. He did not think much of Dolly who had done some fashion designing course after barely scraping through her twelfth exams. Sukhcharan was not opposed to Dolly's modest background but to her mediocre intellectual capabilities and shallow nature.

After marriage, Dolly was soon introduced to page-three socialites and high-society women by Sahbaaz's sisters and cousins. Most of these women were anyway very keen to be friends with her because of her wealthy family background. She was told by her so-called 'mentors' that she should stick by these unwritten rules, if she wanted to climb the social ladder: create a suitable background for herself, learn how to promote herself, become interested in expensive and exclusive stuff, break the nouveau-riche stereotype, be sophisticated, travel and socialize extensively and learn to deal with malicious gossip.

It did not take long for Dolly to be included in their inner circle and soon, she was one of them. They drank expensive wines, attended kitty parties, and went on shopping sprees, extravagant cruises and foreign vacations. Popularly known as socialites, they would assume assorted avatars. They partied for the sake of partying and to keep ennui away. They had no real identities or purpose, only pseudonyms like Mrs. Ahluwalia, music baron's mistress, hotel heiress, social butterfly. They gossiped, preoccupied with the petty trivia of other people and their lives. They appeared everywhere with their trademark fake smiles and air-kisses: at weddings and funerals, feasts and festivals, music launches and art exhibitions.

Dolly was so lost in her world that she had little or no time for her family. This went on for a year after her wedding, until she realised that she was pregnant with her first child. All hell broke loose as she wanted to enjoy her new life without the 'burden' of kids for some more time. She was having a whale of a time since the day she got married and entered 'Ahluwalia Niwas'. She wanted to have an abortion but was severely reprimanded by Sahbaaz for even thinking about it. Dolly had no choice but to go ahead with this unplanned occurrence.

In November 1989, Dolly gave birth to a baby boy. He was named Gurkeerat which means 'one who sings praises of the Lord' and affectionately called Guri. Guri was greatly pampered by his grandfather and father. Dolly was a little 'too busy' to attend to her son and had employed three full time maids to take care of him.

Soon Dolly was back to her normal routine of socializing and partying. Now that she was a mother and ten kilograms heavier, she was expected to graduate from a 'pretty newly-wed' to a 'sophisticated lady'. Just like her new friends, who suddenly assumed random titles like wedding planner, art dealer, and business advisor, Dolly started introducing herself as a fashion consultant and whipped out a business card with a fancy logo and her husband's office address.

Four years after Guri's birth, Dolly was pregnant with her second child. This time, she wanted to make sure she didn't gain any extra weight as she did the first time. She enrolled herself in yoga classes, visited birth consultants, ignored her food cravings and went on a strict diet. Despite a lot of opposition from her husband and parents-in-laws, she refused to budge and continued with her tactics to avoid any weight gain. As feared by the family, Dolly gave birth to a weak baby girl who weighed just about 1.8 kilograms at birth. She was categorized as a 'low birth-weight baby' and needed specialized neonatal care for several weeks after her birth. The girl was named Loveleen and was fondly referred to as Baby by all. The entire family prayed for Baby's well being and quick recovery. Dolly surprised everybody by attending a popular cosmetic store launch party on the sixth day after the baby's birth, looking as slim as before.

Meanwhile, Baby started recovering but she turned out to be

a weak girl with fragile bones, a slight build and short stature, despite having the good Ahluwalia genes.

From the day Baby was born the relationship between Sahbaaz and Dolly started spiralling downwards. Sahbaaz was heartbroken and couldn't believe what was happening. On the surface they appeared cordial but there was major trouble brewing in their relationship. Dolly was never the life partner Sahbaaz had expected her to be. She was a careless wife and an uncaring mother. His father's worst fears had proven right. Shahbaaz thought she had no real purpose in life but to squander his family's hard earned money. She was the most pretentious and emotionally hollow person one could meet. The Dolly, Sahbaaz had fallen in love with, was long since gone. Ever so often, he felt his father's words echo in his ears.

"*Beta*, she is not the right girl for you."

"I have met enough people in my life to tell you that this girl is not good for you."

"She is nothing more than a mere gold digger who is in this relationship only for the money and the luxuries attached to it. Trust me son!"

"I am not getting a good feeling about this girl, *puttar*... Rest is your wish."

Of course, Sahbaaz was too much in love with Dolly at the time to pay heed to his father's advice.

≈

By 2009, 'Ahluwalia Niwas' had just four family members, Sahbaaz, Dolly, Guri and Baby. Chauffeurs, cooks, butlers, gardeners, care-takers and attendants were all over the place. Though he was fond of cars, Sahbaaz preferred to keep just one car for himself at a time. He had bought himself an Audi R8 earlier in the year and planned to keep it for at least another three years. Dolly liked to change her car almost every year depending on what other women in her group bought. She wanted to stay one notch higher than her friends. She bought a Porsche 911 and Lamborghini Gallardo for herself and gifted a Porsche Carrera to Guri when he turned nineteen.

Guri had turned out to be quite a good looking lad. Six feet tall, endowed with a good built and chocolate hero looks, he was immensely popular with the girls. He was sent to a boarding school in Ajmer when he was ten and came back to join St. Stephen's College in Delhi University. Dolly was already being bombarded with marriage proposals for Guri, a fact she took immense pride in.

Guri had nothing in common with his mother and sister. He often told his father that he felt like a 'showpiece' when he was with his mother and that how she left no stone unturned to showcase him in front of her friends.

As for Baby, everybody had nothing but sympathy for Guri's poor little sister. She looked perpetually sick with dark circles under her eyes and pimples on her face. Her mother constantly tried to hide her from her friends. She seemed to be embarrassed about her daughter, though a lot of people gossiped behind her back that she was the one responsible for what Baby had turned out to be.

Baby had always been the butt of all jokes at school and suffered from low self-esteem and eating disorders. In fact, Dolly would shower more attention on her three dogs, a Chinese Pekinese, American Beagle and a French Poodle than her own daughter!

≈

May 1, 2009 was a big day for Sahbaaz. His company, Swari Construction Private Limited, had collaborated with one of the biggest construction companies of the world PSS Global, and today was the launch of the first joint project, a 525-acre township on the outskirts of Noida called "Nova County". Dolly was told that PSS Global was owned by a person of Indian origin who was regularly featured among the richest persons in the world.

Sahbaaz's invitees included politicians, diplomatic envoys, corporate honchos, media tycoons, Bollywood superstars, while Dolly's guest list included socialites with botoxed exteriors, mamma's boys and daddy's girls, ubiquitous small time models and wannabe starlets.

Though it appeared to be like another top notch social event, Dolly knew that tonight was going to be different. It was an international corporate event and she would be on the dias. Dolly was as excited as she had been when she was first introduced to the whole party circuit years ago.

The stage was set and the event would start anytime now. Dolly, standing with her close bunch of friends, declared in her usual high pitched bragging tone, "Oh darlings! I am so incredibly late as usual. I will be called on the stage anytime now. I better rush or the poor guests will have to wait for me unnecessarily."

As she turned to head towards the stage, the floor seemed to give away from under her feet!

There she was. The bitch! Meghna Ahuja.

Dolly had been hearing rumours of Sahbaaz showing undue interest in Meghna which she dismissed with a laugh, "Yeah right! Meghna was kicked out of the scene long time back when Mr. Ahluwalia selected me and not her! I don't give a rat's ass if she is still desperate to win him back. I know my husband well enough... This Meghna Veghna is a nobody, okay?"

Hell! No! Meghna was unveiling the project on the stage. She couldn't believe her eyes. How could Sahbaaz do this?

Other than Sahbaaz and Meghna, there were two foreigners and one Indian on the stage. Sahbaaz took the mike and introduced Ronald Harris and Stephen Marshall, the CEO and the Project Head respectively. As he started to introduce the distinguished looking guy, most probably from the Indian subcontinent, Dolly's good friend Shelly Khanna tapped her on the shoulder and said cheerfully "Hiiiiiiiiiiii!!!!! I was looking for you on the stage but am surprised to find you here!! What happened?"

Dolly smiled weakly and said, "Well...mmmm...excuse me... ahem...mm...I have to go please!" Shelly stood there smirking. She had got enough fodder today to gossip for a month at least. Dolly Ahluwalia looking all flushed while Meghna Ahuja shared the stage with her husband, Sahbaaz 'Moneybags' Ahluwalia.

Red-faced, Dolly rushed to the refuge of the washroom as there were too many eyes staring at her while she had nothing to say. She was on the verge of crying but managed to compose herself and come back to the party. The stage ceremony was almost over and drinks were being served. She walked towards Sahbaaz who was standing with the 'distinguished looking guy', Meghna and other guests. He knew what Dolly was going to ask and quickly stepped away from the group.

"What the bloody hell is this Sahbaaz?" asked Dolly seething in anger.

"What exactly are you talking about?" asked Sahbaaz, raising his brows.

"You know bloody well what I am talking about," retorted Dolly.

"Oh Meghna...Listen. What Meghna is doing here is none of your business. She will be heading this joint venture from our side. This is a decision taken by the board of directors," explained Sahbaaaz very matter-of-factly.

A starlet wearing a revealing outfit with a daringly low neckline and a high hemline waved at Dolly.

"And thanks for inviting these bunch of jokers to this important function," he added sarcastically looking at the starlet.

As he was about to turn away from red-with-anger Dolly, Sahbaaz noticed Mr. Saini, the chairman of PSS Global, popularly known as PS in business circles, approaching them. Sahbaaz smiled at

Mr. Saini and said, "Oh Mr. Saini, let me introduce you to Dolly... She is..."

His voice trailed off as he saw Dolly staring wide-eyed at Mr. Saini.

"Oh! I see. Somebody has already introduced you to each other it seems. Good!" said Sahbaaz thinking they had been introduced earlier in the party.

Dolly had recognized him!

Pratyaksh Singh Saini, the Indian-American businessman and philanthropist, the chairman and co-founder of PSS Global, a Fortune 500 company. He had received a Bachelor of Technology degree in Mechanical Engineering from the Indian Institute of Technology, Bombay followed by an MBA in Finance from the Indian Institute of Management, Ahmedabad. He was offered plum jobs by leading companies of the world. But he declined them all and went on to start a business analytics company PSS Analytics in the United States with a close friend and an IIM-A batch mate.

Today, he ranked in all prominent lists of the rich and the powerful.

"Top 10 Richest People in the World".

"Top 50 Most Powerful Personalities".

"Top Newsmakers of the Year".

"Hi Dolly! Do I know you?" asked Pratyaksh in a thick American accent.

Pratyaksh failed to recognize his childhood crush, Davinder. He could not be blamed. Dolly was unrecognizable in her present avatar with her blonde hair, nose job, pumped-up lips and botoxed face.

Dolly stared blankly at Pratyaksh as Sahbaaz walked towards Meghna and greeted her with a hug and a peck on her cheek.

Desi Hip Hop King

He steps out of his white limousine wearing a skin-tight white shirt which accentuates his biceps and narrow-fit orange trousers with a chunky metallic belt. A long gold chain with a *khanda* dangles on his chest. (*Khanda* is a double-edged sword and an important part of the design of the Sikh national flag, called the Nishan Sahib.) He is wearing white and gold Emporio Armani shades, a diamond stud in his left ear and a glittering, sequin studded turban on his head.

As he steps out, a battery of photographers and journalists lunge towards him with their cameras and microphones.

Flash! Flash! Flash! Blah! Blah! Blah! Flash! Blah! Blah! Flash!

Suddenly, all at once, everybody is talking.

It's a pleasant October evening in 2009. The noise is eardrum-shattering. The light is blinding. His personal bodyguards and the organizer's security personnel start pushing everybody back to make way for him. He starts walking towards the stage with a distinct swagger that only he can do. Suddenly as if out of nowhere, five men in black suits appear. They are the event organizers, managers, sycophants and sponsors.

They greet him. He doesn't reply. They ask questions. He answers with a nonchalant nod of his head or a wave of the hand.

He starts walking briskly towards the stage, half hopping and half running. The cheers, shrieks, catcalls and whistles become louder and louder...

A voice over the speaker system announces, *"Mundeyon te kudiyon*...ladies and gentlemen...give it up for the one and only... Jaaaeeeeeeeeee--keeeeeeeeey S...S...S...Jacky S!"

The noise has reached a deafening level. The crowd starts yelling... Jacky...Jacky...Jacky…

In one stride he climbs onto the stage and starts jumping and waving to the crowd of more than fifty thousand, a sea of heads and arms.

Jacky...Jacky...Jacky...

A mike is flung onto the stage. He catches it. The stage lights go off. The crowd falls silent. A spotlight appears and randomly moves on the stage. Left to right and right to left.

A few seconds later, the spotlight focusses on him. The crowd roars again!

Jacky...Jacky...Jacky...

He starts singing in his now-trademark high pitch voice. The crowd goes berserk. The stage lights are turned on.

He is lip syncing to the song which is being played in the background.

He 'sings' four of his popular tracks one after the other, "*Jaan meri tu*" (you are my life), "*O mitro ajj bhangda pauna aa*" (hey friends, we have to dance tonight), "*dil tuteya aa mera*" (my heart is broken) and "*waheguru tu dhan hai*" (god, you are great).

Like other popular Punjabi pop singers, he has one song in each of these categories: praising-a-girl song, chilling-with-your-friends song, broken-heart song, praising-the-Almighty song.

The performance lasts for twenty minutes. The crowd chants 'Once more! Once more!' but in vain. The stage lights go off.

Jacky S's performance was supposed to be the highlight of the popular awards show, "Channel P Awards Night 2009". According to the contract, the performance duration was to be twenty minutes. So there he was, off the stage precisely twenty minutes after he started. His manager Randeep (who also happens to be his cousin) sends his make-up artist Raghu near the left edge of the stage to signal the same, exactly five minutes before he was supposed to end his performance.

≈

Jagdeep Singh Sekhon was born into a middle class family in Jalandhar on March 10, 1989. His father was employed with the State Bank of India while his mother was a government school teacher. Jagdeep was born after a long wait of ten years. Being the only son, Jagdeep, was always under great pressure from his parents to study hard and become an IAS officer.

Though he was a good student, he somehow did not see himself as an IAS officer or a doctor or an engineer for that matter.

His mother Govind Kaur, who came from a religious family, wanted him to learn religious hymns called *'gurbani'* at the local gurudwara. From the age of eight, he would be packed off to the gurudwara as soon as he would return from school.

The Babaji or the head priest at the gurudwara, Bhai Gulbagh Singh Jalandharwaale saw a lot of spark in Jagdeep. He taught him to play the harmonium. And Jagdeep surprised everybody by picking it up really fast! The pump organ or harmonium is a type of reed organ that generates sound with hand-pumped bellows.

Babaji could see that the boy was a natural when it came to music. He was not only a quick learner but also a passionate one. Confident of his talent, Babaji started teaching him *gurbani* in 'classical raag' format.

Jagdeep's parents were oblivious to this talent and just wanted him to learn *gurbani* in a basic format. That had been a part of their growing up years and they wanted their son, too, to learn it.

On the auspicious day of *Gurpurab*, his parents were in for a surprise. As they walked into the gurudwara and sat down after bowing down to the *Guru Granth Sahib*, the religious book of the Sikhs, they saw their young son Jagdeep sitting on the dais with a tabla player and a harmonium player on either side. He was wearing a white kurta pyjama paired with an orange turban, repeatedly adjusting his small harmonium.

The parents were in tears as they felt an overwhelming sense of emotion and pride looking at their son in this Sikhi attire. This was one of the proudest moments of their lives. As they composed themselves, he started singing *"Tu samrath sada hum deen bhikhari Ram"*. (You are eternal and all-powerful; I am a mere beggar, O Ram.)

His melodious voice was sweet as honey and his tune was perfection personified. He started his second hymn, *"Lakh khushiyan patshaiyan je satguru nadr kare"* (Hundreds of thousands of princely pleasures are enjoyed, if the true Guru bestows His glance of grace).

The crowd was unusually silent as if mesmerized by his angelic voice!

After the *ardaas* (a Sikh prayer done after completion of a religious function) and *langar* (food served to the visitors in a gurudwara) the crowd gathered around Jagdeep. He could not quite comprehend what this attention was about! All he wanted to do was go home and play with his friends.

While his parents stood around talking about the event and the appreciation they received for their son, Jagdeep quietly sneaked away to play *bandar killa*, his favorite game, with his friends. *Bandar killa* (monkey's fort) is a local game played by four or more children. First the children do a *pugun pugayee*, a kind of toss without a coin. The one who loses the *pugun pugayee* becomes the *bandar* i.e. monkey. A circle is drawn on the ground and every player places his or her footwear (usually slippers) in the circle. Then the *bandar* stands in the middle of the circle and all the other players have to steal the slippers from the circle without being caught. If the *bandar* touches a player while he is stealing, then that player becomes the *bandar*. If the *bandar* can't get hold of anyone and everyone gets away with their pair of slippers, then he loses the game and is bombarded by the same slippers as he runs to touch a pre-decided spot on a nearby wall to avoid being further hit!

It surely was Jagdeep's lucky day as he didn't lose even once and mercilessly hurled slippers at his friends. After the game was over, he walked to a nearby video parlour with his best friend, Bunty, to play video games. The owner charged five rupees for a game of twenty minutes. As he sat down to play the game, a group of boys sitting on the next console started pointing at Jagdeep and commenting about his performance at the gurudwara in the morning.

A pimply-faced teenaged boy, commented, "Hey! Look! The new *Babaji* in the town is playing video games! Hahahahaha..." and the boys burst into laughter.

Jagdeep ignored them. Bunty asked "What are they talking about Deepya?"

"I performed at the gurudwara today," he replied with a straight face concentrating on his game

"Oh I see, but..."

"*Arre*...You concentrate on the game *na!*" Jagdeep, visibly irritated with the conversation, cut him short as he tried to say something.

It seemed singing religious hymns in a gurudwara was not a cool thing to do for kids who were rapidly getting exposed to the world of TV, video games and disco songs.

≈

While his parents were making grand plans of enrolling him in a professional singing class, Jagdeep had other plans. He made it amply clear to his parents that he was only interested in studying and nothing else. After his mother's tearful persistence and pleading, he reluctantly agreed that he would continue learning music in the gurudwara but would not perform in any religious or public function as he found it too distracting! His parents had indulged him since childhood and now had no other option but to agree to his demands this time as well.

Despite all this pretence, Jagdeep knew that he actually wanted to be a singer. But he had decided that he would wait for the right time and opportunity.

≈

As he turned sixteen Jagdeep became increasingly interested in pop music. He was in awe of Bhangra hip-hop singers like Bally Sagoo and Dr. Zeus who were ruling the popularity charts. At the same time he had tremendous respect for Punjabi singers such as Harbhajan Mann and Hans Raj Hans when it came to actual singing skills.

His mother did not like his new obsession and would often try to discourage him against this hip-hop trend. She wanted him to become a Punjabi folk singer like Gurdas Mann, if not a religious one. But he wanted to be like one of those foreign bred artists who wore fancy clothes and rapped between their lines. He called them the 'Yo' singers and would emulate them.

By the time he reached high school, he started composing his own songs and performing at school functions.

On one such function in January 2005, he was discovered by the renowned music producer, Gurvinder Kohli, who was invited for their school's Annual Day function as the chief guest. Jagdeep's performance was the highlight of the show. Gurvinder Kohli was amazed to see how good this teenager was.

After the show, he gave Jagdeep his number and told him to come to his studio in Chandigarh. Jagdeep kept this a secret from his parents. He travelled to Chandigarh on the pretext of joining a coaching class for an engineering entrance exam. His parents arranged accommodation for him as a paying guest and also gave him his first mobile phone so that they could be in touch with him.

The next day he met Gurvinder Kohli, or Kohli Sahab as he was popularly called in the music fraternity, in his recording studio. This was Jagdeep's first professional audition. And he wanted it to be the last!

As he walked into the studio, he was thrilled to see what he had always dreamt of. A big fancy control room with mixing consoles, recorders, synthesizers and monitors, isolation booths, drums, electric guitars.

But Jagdeep was not the one to get overwhelmed by all this. He was a confident boy with big dreams and was definitely not going to buckle under pressure.

Kohli Sahab was not alone. There were at least five other people in the control room besides the technician.

The song he had prepared for today's audition was called *"Jaan meri tu"*. This was a tried and tested song as he had received tremendous adulation when he sung this song at a local event a month ago. This time, he was going to present a refined version of the same, which he reckoned would definitely impress them.

He confidently entered the singing booth and took to the microphone like a seasoned professional. He closed his eyes and started the song at a high pitch. When he finished the song and opened his eyes he could see wide smiles on everyone's faces. He had never felt so relieved ever before in his life!

Kohli Sahab congratulated him with a warm hug and told him to come the next day to sign the contract for his first music album.

Jagdeep was over the moon. He called his mother to break this good news. She was ecstatic despite the fact that her son had lied to her to get his way. She forgave him and left for Chandigarh along with his father.

The next day, Jagdeep signed on the contract in the presence of his parents. They went to the nearest gurudwara to pay obeisance and thank God for this good news.

The only thing his parents were against was the renaming of their son by Kohli Sahab and his team. They had rechristened him Jacky S.

~

On October 28, 2006, Jagdeep's or rather Jacky S's first album was released amid great fanfare and an advertising blitzkrieg. Kohli Sahiab left no stone unturned to ensure that this album broke all previous records and created a benchmark in Punjabi pop music industry.

And it did ! The album went on to create history. It became the highest selling album in Punjabi music industry and the title song *"Jaan meri tu"* was declared a country wide hit. It was the most frequently played song in clubs and lounges in cities as far as Mumbai and Bangalore.

Seventeen-year old Jacky S became an overnight sensation. Suddenly, everyone wanted a piece of this new pop star. The media started camping outside his house in Jalandhar. The phone rang incessantly. Advertisers vied to sign him to promote their brands and products. He was a rage amongst the girls with his unconventional looks and great style. Whatever he wore became an instant fashion.

Acquaintances became friends. Friends became best friends. Best friends became brothers.

He hired a public relations firm and a management agency to take care of his image and handle his day-to-day operations. He was advised to develop a trademark dressing style. After careful deliberation, his look was finalized. It was rock-meets-funk style with colourful clothes and metallic accessories.

He released three albums each year which would all be sold out the moment they arrived on the shelves. Such was the Jacky S mania. He was all over the place, from TV to hoardings and from T-shirts to mugs.

The more successful he became, the faster his moral values declined. He did not realize when he transformed from being an ambitious middle class teenager, who was close to his roots, to a conceited and depraved pop star who liked to surround himself with sychophants. He started drifting away from his parents. Calls to the family became fewer by the day. Nights were now spent in the company of wannabe models, a different one every night.

He started hanging out in the company of fraudsters, drug addicts and corrupt businessmen. He would instruct his team to run defamatory online campaigns against upcoming singers. Desperate to nip competition in the bud, he started negotiating exclusive contracts with music labels to ensure that budding singers stood no chance.

He outdid himself when he back-stabbed Kohli Sahab at the last moment and instead tied up with a rival music label for just a little more money.

Jacky S aspired to be an actor and launched his own production company by the name of Jacky Entertainment Pvt. Ltd in the latter half of 2010 and was in talks with financiers to fund his maiden movie, which was speculated to be a high budget historical drama where he was to play Maharaja Ranjit Singh.

≈

But in the summer of 2011, suddenly the bubble burst. An infamous drug mafia don Raja Sodhi named Jacky S as one of his regular customers after he was arrested for organizing a rave party in Manali. More than twenty people died in that party. The case became an overnight national issue.

Overnight the media's darling suddenly became the media's latest victim. Rivals pounced on him with vicious aggression. Advertisers dumped him. Best friends, friends and acquaintances just melted away.

"Hip-Hop King Jacky S involved in the Manali drug scandal!" screamed the headline in a leading English newspaper.

"Jacky S should be sent to jail!" a popular Punjabi newspaper declared, convicting him before the trial had even begun. Jacky's team had failed to give enough print advertisement space to this particular Punjabi newspaper during the release of his last album. The newspaper management had secretly vowed to get back at an appropriate time; and now it was their time.

≈

Jagdeep was in shock from the moment this news broke out. It had been a week ever since and there seemed to be no way out of this mess. He had locked himself in his Chandigarh house and sent away all his staff. Sitting all alone, he alternated between crying and sleeping.

He was missing his parents terribly. He picked up his personal mobile and thought of calling his mother but suddenly felt too embarrassed and ashamed. What would he tell his parents now? How would his mother react? Had it been anything else, but the drugs, it would have been still manageable. They would have disowned me by now. I don't know what explanation they would be giving to their relatives, he thought to himself.

Suddenly he saw his mother's number blinking on his phone! He pressed the green button.

How he had been waiting to hear her voice. "Hello son !"

He managed a weak hello in reply.

"I know you must be busy. Just wanted to tell you that both of us here know that you are not involved in this drug scandal. Don't worry. *Waheguru* is with you."

He choked up with emotion and started sobbing inconsolably. Everyone, but his parents, was convinced that he was involved in this.

The truth was that he wasn't.

His association with Raja Sodhi was purely for business. Jacky S had approached Raja Sodhi to fund his upcoming movie venture. Raja had agreed and a grand launch was organized. A couple of days before the shooting was to begin, Raja tried to re-negotiate since he wanted a larger share in the movie's profits. Jacky not only refused but approached another financier for his movie and cancelled the agreement with Raja, who then threatened him with dire consequences. And here he was, facing the consequences of that.

Jagdeep wiped his tears and felt he was ready to face the world again. He felt as if somebody had pumped life into his lifeless body after days of great mental torture. It was unbelievable how a few words from his mother could give him so much confidence.

To hell with the world from now on, he thought.

He had learnt the hard way that at the end of the day it would be just his family that would stand with him, no matter what happened.

≈

Detailed police investigations finally revealed that Jacky S had nothing to do with the scandal and was dragged into this controversy because of Raja Sodhi's ulterior motives.

The same media which had painted him in the vilest of colours lost no time in welcoming him back to his rightful place.

"Jacky S is back with a bang!" declared the English newspaper headline.

"The police investigations have revealed that singer Jacky S's name was dragged into this controversy unnecessarily and he has nothing to do with the entire drug episode. Additional charges of misleading the investigations to be slapped on Raja Sodhi." This was found as a part of a small article on page eight in the popular Punjabi newspaper.

Slowly, his life appeared to be back on track.

The music fraternity welcomed him with open arms again. Rivals kept their mouths shut. The advertisers came back and that too with a public apology. Best friends, friends and acquaintances appeared out of blue with varied excuses justifying their disappearance.

Life became normal again, but one thing changed.

His attitude towards life.

Wanted - An NRI Groom

"Do you know how to cook?"

"A little bit..."

"Hmm..Do you know how to knit?"

"No."

"Do you go to the Gurudwara?"

"Sometimes."

"What do you like to do in your spare time?"

"I just do fun-*shun* with my friends."

"Fun-*shun*! What is fun-*shun*? How do you do fun-*shun*?"

"Fun-*shun*, you know...chilling out...regular stuff like that."

"Oh!...Regular stuff like what?"

"Driving around on my scooter, going to coffee shops, you know."

"Hmm..."

A long and awkward silence; typical of a situation when everybody in the room either looks around uncomfortably or just quietly sips tea.

"Mrs. Dhaliwal...It was nice meeting your daughter. We will connect with you over the phone by Wednesday. Hope that's okay with you."

"Sure. Sure. Not a problem. We will eagerly await your phone call."

"Ok ji...We will take your leave now."

If you are wondering whether this is an excerpt from a job interview, it is not. It is an interview albeit of a different kind. This conversation took place just half an hour ago between my prospective mother-in-law Mrs. Mangat and me. Before you laugh it off as a one-off incident, let me tell you this is a conversation which has become a regular feature of my life since the last one year. Let me give you a background before I flood you with my stories and funny tidbits. Gee... I just love talking.

Hi Diary,

I am Sukhmanpreet (yes, that's just my first name) Kaur Dhaliwal. SMP or Preeti in short. My mom wanted to name me Sukhman and my dad liked the name Manpreet. As always, they couldn't agree and so decided to name me Sukhmanpreet instead.

What the hell.

Now I have to live with this name all my life. I have been harbouring secret plans of getting my name changed to Preity. You know like Preity Zinta, the Bollywood actress. Preity Dhaliwal. How cool will that be!

Anyway, I am twenty three years old. Fair. Tall (if 5'7" is tall for you). Neither fat nor thin (Psst...used to be fat as a teenager but now am cool). Not-so-intelligent but street smart, as they call it. Well behaved (well...mostly). I love my parents and hate my brother. I have or rather, had a group of five close friends (three girls, Niyati, Gaganjeet, Sonam and two boys Amanjot and Yashvir). We have been together since childhood. All the three girls are married.. Niyati and Sonam are in Delhi and Gaganjeet is in Canada. Amanjot is married too and lives in Amritsar itself. Will come to the fifth one, Yashvir later. ;-)

We live in Putligarh area of Amritsar, the spiritual and cultural capital of Punjab.

My father runs a hardware business. Hardware, as in sanitary-hardware not computer-hardware. My mom runs a fashion boutique by the name of 'Fashion Diva Boutique'. She manages to earn just enough to take care of our basic monthly household expenses.

Pssst..Her boutique is pretty popular in our locality though I am not a big fan of her designs. They are too gaudy for my taste. Big flowers. Fancy lace. Heavy embroidery and sequins. I like simple and elegant stuff.

My brother Balkarandeep (Yes, it is the same story again!) or Karan is three years younger to me but is a major pain in the ass. I hate him and the feeling is mutual. We studied in the same school since childhood. Before I proceed, a gentle warning to all parents.

Please...Oh...Please...don't ever put your kids in the same school. Never...especially if they don't get along well. It is not healthy. They just can't enjoy their life. It hampers their social life...everything gets reported back home. It's a clear breach of privacy...I hope you get my point.

My parents have been looking for a suitable groom for me since the day I graduated last year. I wouldn't say I am against marriage. I too want to get married and have been dreaming of it since the last ten years.

Like most girls in Punjab, I just love everything about marriages. Clothes. Make-up. Jewellery. Traditions. *Baraat*. Dancing. *Chhed Chhaad*. Name it and I love it.

My cousins from Bombay can't understand our obsession with marriages, especially our own. But for us here in Amritsar, we just love it and look forward to it. And again, like most other girls in Punjab, I want to get married to an NRI (Non-Resident Indian) boy. And ditto for my parents. They too want me to get hitched to an NRI boy. Ah! Thank God we agree on something at least.

My father has two siblings, a brother, Gurmeet and a sister, Surinder; and both of them are settled abroad. Gurmeet *Chachaji* went to the US as a seventeen year old and settled there for good. My paternal aunt, Surinder *Bhuaji* got married to an NRI boy from Australia a week before her high school final exams. *Ki farak painda hai!* (What difference does it make!) My grandparents would casually remark when asked about their daughter not writing her exam and getting married instead. My dad had never wanted to go abroad and he decided to settle in Amritsar.

But eight years ago, he had a change of heart. His shop was doing well and he wanted to expand his business for which he wanted a loan of fifteen lakh rupees. My mother too gave her approval, which doesn't happen often in our house. The necessary documents were readied. All he needed to do now was approach a few banks and get the loan approved.

But little did he imagine that he would have to run from pillar to post just for this small business loan. Having been born and brought up in India, he had faced corruption in his everyday routine, but I guess life had taken a heavy toll on him by this time. He was a thirty nine year old helpless, middle class man bringing up two kids in a small city. He approached all the banks and financial institutions offering loan in the city. They were not interested in the documents or the profile. They just wanted a bribe for approving the loan. Every evening my father would come home with a dejected look on his face and the same story. My father was a principled man who did not believe in taking shortcuts in life or cheating someone. To cut the long story short, he did not get that loan he so wanted.

After this particular incident, the bitter realities of life became starkly clear. Small incidents which were earlier ignored or dismissed as 'whatever' now became a regular point of heated discussion in our house.

Of course, the fact that both *Chachaji's* and *Bhuaji's* families were doing extraordinarily well did not help. My father started to believe that he made a mistake when he had decided against moving abroad in his youth.

I don't know whether he was right or wrong. But, ever since I can remember I for sure knew that I wanted to settle abroad. I don't care about money or career. I just want to live a good life. And living here in Amritsar is not going to help me do that.

'Girls shouldn't go out so much.'

'Boys are the future of the family.'

'Don't wear short tops.'

'Don't hang around with boys.'

'What will the neighbours say?'

'Girls are not supposed to do this.'

'We can't afford it.'

I just hate this. All these preachy lines are so annoying but I have to listen to them day in and day out. And this is definitely not the life I want for myself.

So, the plan is that I should get married to some decent-looking, decent-earning NRI guy, who is a permanent resident (PR, Green Card holder whatever they call it) or a citizen of US, Australia, Canada so that I get a PR automatically on the basis of marriage and then I invite my parents and brother there. My brother then pursues his higher studies there and gets a decent job. And everybody is together. Happily ever after.

I have a couple of countries on my priority list. I would love to go to America. Canada is cool too. Australia is okay. UK and New Zealand are 'whatever'. And ditto for most of the European countries and South-East Asian countries though I am open to them if there is no other option.

No, I haven't been to any of these countries. And my choices are based on internet information, especially Facebook pictures of my cousins. I am so bloody jealous of them.

This diary thing is fun. Niyati was right. I should have started doing this much earlier.

I am sleepy now. Will catcha later. Wait....am supposed to sign and write today's date and time.

Love,

P. Dhaliwal

5th June 2012. 2150hrs.

P.S. My signature sucks. Gotta change it. Damn.

~

Hi Diary,

Got up late today. Mom had to practically drag me out of bed. I love sleeping till late. My mom says I need to get my act straightened out as soon as possible.

"What will your mother-in-law think if you sleep this late in your new house after marriage?"

"*Arre*...After marriage I will get up early. Let me enjoy here at least, mom."

"Get up quickly and help me in the kitchen. Your in-laws will think that I haven't taught you anything."

"Ok..I will get up. When are the Sandhus coming? Is their son coming along as well?"

"They are coming at five in the evening. Rest I don't know. I don't want to call them again and again. They will think we are too eager for this to work out."

"Ok...Ok...fine...Which suit should I wear? The peach one?"

"No! No! Don't wear that. We never get past the first meeting whenever you wear it. Throw it away..."

"Mmmmm...Ok...I will wear the blue one."

"No. You wear some nice kurti with jeans. This family is quite modern. They will not like a girl in salwar-kameez"

"Ok...fine...I will wear my sleeveless pink kurti."

"Yes. That should be fine. And leave your hair open."

"Ok...Mom...I love you."

"I just pray to God something good works out soon."

My poor mom is running out of patience, especially after my

friend Gaganjeet's wedding. She got married to a boy from Ottawa in Canada. He works as a hardware engineer or something. Gaganjeet is a pretty girl. 5'10". Thin. Super fair. Sharp features. And this boy is really weird. He is 5'8", dark and fat. They make an odd couple. Anyway, Gaganjeet is really happy so it's okay, I guess.

The family that is coming today to see me is family number seventeen. The boy's father had shifted to Australia as a teenager. The boy coming to see me is their only son. They are looking for a modern but homely girl. I have seen his pictures and he looks good.

The Sandhus arrived sharp at five in a rented Skoda Superb. Not bad. There were five people in all. Mr. Sandhu, Mrs. Sandhu, Mr. Sandhu's brother and his Malaysian wife. And of course, the boy, Simar.

Sandhus were one hell of a good looking family. Mrs. Sandhu looked like a queen, with her fancy pyjama suit and pearl necklace. I was so sure they would reject me. I looked like a plain Jane in front of them.

After the usual rounds of tea, snacks, cold drinks I stepped in wearing my favourite pink kurti. I greeted everyone and sat down.

All of them except the boy 'interviewed' me. The boy did not utter a single word. In fact, he looked bored. He looked better in person than in the photos. He must be 6'2", fair, well built and strikingly handsome.

His parents seemed to like me. Mrs. Sandhu asked her son if he wanted to ask me anything in private. He just stared at his mother, which the mother took as an affirmative. She asked my parents if her son could chat with me separately. My folks readily agreed.

I got up and walked towards my room hoping he would follow me. While entering my room, I looked at him from the corner of my eye. It seemed to me that he wasn't too keen but nevertheless he got up and followed me to my room.

Entering the room, he sat on a couch and started looking around casually.

"Hi Simar, I am Preeti," I said.

"Hi Preeti," he replied in a bored voice.

He spoke with a thick Australian accent. I love people with an accent.

"Umm..Is there anything you want to ask me or something?"

"Not really, Preeti."

He sounded sarcastic.

"Oh...Uh...Ok..."

I composed myself and said, "If you don't like me we can just go out. You can tell your parents. Let them figure it out then."

"Ok..."

He got up as he said that.

I don't know what got into my head but as he was stepping out, I blurted, "Simar, you are really rude!"

"Excuse me!"

"You are really rude," I said.

"And why is that?"

"Ask yourself. If you didn't like me, you could have just said that politely. Or could have engaged in a casual conversation and then gone home and told your parents. It's not like my parents were forcing your family to decide immediately."

"Ok. Let me cut this short. I am not into girls. My parents know that and they still want me to marry an Indian girl. I have a boyfriend back home."

Holy mother of all Gods!

He stormed out and I just stood there speechless. Very quietly, I closed the door, jumped on my bed, hid my face under a pillow and burst out laughing. This was one of the funniest things that had ever happened to me. I just couldn't believe it.

Finally, I got up, collected myself and walked out of my room. As I entered the drawing room everybody had their eyes on me. I entered and sat down, adjusting my hair.

Mrs. Sandhu looked confused. I think she figured out what had happened in my room.

"Ok. M...M...Mrs. Dhaliwal. We will get back to you on this by tomorrow, if that's o...o...ok with you."

"Sure, Mrs. Sandhu. It was a pleasure meeting you and your family. I hope everything works out."

"Same here, Mrs. Dhaliwal."

The moment their car went out of sight, my parents dragged me inside the house. All three of them looked at me expectantly.

"He look like a movie star!" my brother was the first one to speak.

"Mrs. Sandhu said she really liked you and that you were exactly what they were looking for," said my mom, almost choking with happiness.

"What difference does that make if Mrs. Sandhu likes me," I retorted.

"Why??!!" my mother said, her expression changing from super-thrilled to what-the-hell!

I fell on to the sofa and burst out laughing loudly.

"Preeti, the boy didn't like you or what? What happened inside?" my mom asked. Now her face had that speak-up-girl-or-I-will-throttle-you-to-death expression.

"Mom, he didn't like me. And for that matter, he wouldn't have liked me even if I was Miss World."

"Why?" my mom, dad and brother asked in unison.

"Why! Because he likes boys and he has a boyfriend. And before you ask me who said this...and how can you say that and stuff like that...let me tell you..He himself told me this."

The moment I uttered these words, my mother just walked out of the room. My dad followed her into the kitchen.

My brother looked at me and started laughing.

"I knew it man..." he said.

"What you knew it? You thought he looked like a movie star *na*!"

"So! Movie stars can't be gay or what!"

"Whatever..."

"This is shit funny, man...Wait till I tell my friends and everybody else."

"Like I care."

My brother is officially the most annoying person in the world.

So, this was today's main story. Seriously *yaar*, what is wrong with all the men in this world.

As if today's incident wasn't enough, my father suddenly got a panic attack late in the evening, a normal occurrence of the last couple of months whenever a prospect backed out.

"Preeti! Open those matrimonial websites on your computer and show me the list of boys immediately."

"Dad, can you please wait for half an hour. Let me eat something at least...I am hungry."

"No! I can't...come here immediately and open those websites... shaadi.com, jeevansaathi.com whatever..."

I clearly had no other option but to do as I was told. Apparently, fifteen minutes ago, my mom had called Mrs. Mangat (yesterday's party, remember?) who said that they were not interested in taking this alliance forward. The reason was unspecified.

So, here we were. My mother, father and me huddled around our old computer trying to find more boys who matched our expectations. I logged on to www.shaadi.com, typed in my id and password. A couple of requests had come, mostly from local good-for-nothing boys. I declined them all.

We put two filters on the search results.

Religion: Sikh

Living in: All but India

Initially, my parents had been adamant about my marrying into our caste Jat, but looking at the current situation, they let go off it. Jats form around sixty per cent of the total Sikh population and my parents didn't want to let go of the remaining forty per cent non-Jats who might be NRIs.

We carefully scanned profiles, expressing interest in the ones we liked. I had put out three of my best photos. My parents wanted me to get a professional portfolio done while I wanted to post a couple of my casual pictures. Of course, I had photo-shopped them. So, eventually, we put two professional and one casual picture. I was looking much prettier in these pictures but so does everybody else. Dark circles, pimple marks were all removed. This is a usual norm, posting pictures in which you look so much better than your real self. Ha! Ha!

We spent long hours scanning profiles and emailing 'candidates' who 'fit the bill'. And so another day got over.

Time to go to sleep now.

Love,

P. Dhaliwal ...

6th June 2012 2200hrs.

~

Hi Diary,

I had weird dreams and a very disturbed sleep last night. I dreamt that I was stranded on some strange island. I was running all over the place and asking for help. I kept on yelling but nobody came. Got up with a severe headache in the morning.

I checked my emails to see if anybody had responded to my requests on the matrimonial websites. There were a couple of new emails but, damnnnnn, they were either spam mails or advertisements for some random services.

Am feeling really low today. I am missing Yashvir a lot. His full name is Yashvir Samra. He was one of my closest friends. Ok. A little more than just a close friend. We were together since kindergarten. God knows when the friendship blossomed into love. I think it happened during our eighth standard class trip to Kullu. He is 5'10" tall and has the cutest dimples ever and is one of the nicest boys you could meet.

He proposed marriage to me after our tenth standard results. I was head over heels in love with him and so I accepted. God!! We were such kids! We meticulously started planning our future. He took the non-medical stream after the tenth while I chose medical. I told him that I wanted to settle abroad only. He was a mediocre student but started studying really hard for SAT, IELTS as well as TOEFL, the tests to be cleared to go abroad.

Around that time, his mother fell seriously ill. After a couple of tests, the doctors diagnosed her with multiple sclerosis, an incurable neuro-disorder. A lot of the family money went into her treatment. Yashvir managed to get good grades but not good enough to get a scholarship. His family advised him to drop the idea of going abroad and instead study in a decent college in India itself.

I understood the situation and told him to do whatever he felt was right, and whatever he chose to do I would stand by his decision. He took admission in a leading engineering college in Patiala.

My parents wanted me to pursue a course in nursing and with my decent scores in the entrance exams, I managed to get admission in a local nursing college. The distance between Patiala and Amritsar coupled with my parents' increasing enthusiasm to send me abroad took a toll on our relationship.

Most of the girls in the BSc nursing course take admission with the dream of eventually settling abroad as there is a huge demand for nurses, especially in the US and Canada. That was the reason my parents insisted on my doing this course in the first place. It was all planned, I guess, and I wouldn't say I was not aware of it. I was hoping everything would somehow work out between me and Yashvir but also the desire to settle abroad was really over-powering.

After his third year final exams, Yashvir came to Amritsar. It was around the same time that my parents had started pestering me to get married. Yashvir and I met at a coffee shop and I told him that there was no future in the relationship. He tried to convince me to change my decision. He begged me to give the relationship one more year and even broke down and started crying. To help him gradually get over me, I told him I would try for six more months, but it was a lie I told him just to make him feel better.

After he left, I gave the go-ahead to my family to start looking for a suitable match for me.

We began by scanning the matrimonial sections of all leading newspapers. Every Thursday we would circle the advertisements that we found suitable, and Friday to Wednesday would be spent telephoning and emailing those shortlisted candidates.

Meanwhile, I decreased the frequency of my phone calls and emails to Yashvir. Things started cooling off between us. Our relationship had almost come to an end by September.

We also started placing advertisements in the matrimonial sections of leading newspapers. We did get responses from a couple of the candidates. Some would talk to you for some time and then suddenly disappear into thin air. Some would just beat around the bush.

Most of these NRIs come to India during the winters, between October to February. We had lined up meetings with around seven to eight of these NRIs. Our schedule was almost full from October to February and we were optimistic something would work out. Since the NRI grooms normally come for a few days the wedding has to be arranged at a short notice. My parents had started shortlisting marriage halls, caterers, printers for the invitation cards and buying gold jewellery.

Now I have got to chat with this guy from London. Will catcha later.

Love,

P. Dhaliwal

7th June 2012. 2145hrs.

~

Hiiiii Diaryyyy,

Sorry, it's been ages...have been so busy last three weeks that there was no time to write. But there is good news! We heard from two boys whom we had met earlier this year. One is from Melbourne in Australia and the other one is from Chicago in US. Both of them are keen on taking this forward. I am more interested in the one from Chicago though the Melbourne one is better looking. I would prefer the US over Australia any day.

Kamalpreet is the one from the US. He went to US about six

years ago after his father's death. His mother lives with him in the US. He is in the transport industry. They didn't quite specify what he actually does but they appear well settled. The best part is that he is the only son. No sisters. No brothers. Cool! My folks are trying to find out more about the boy and his family from our distant relatives who claim to belong to their neighbouring village.

Oh..He is going to call me any moment now. Will catcha later... byeeeeeeeeeeeeeee...

Love,

P. Dhaliwal...

25th June 2012. 2315hrs.

≈

Hiii Diary,

Long time again...sorry...the moment I think my life is on track it gets messy again...am so confused. Kamalpreet stopped responding to my calls...we thought they probably found another girl who is better than me or something. Then, after a week, his maternal uncle from Moga in Punjab called my father and told him that if he wished to take this proposal forward, he would have to give either twenty five lakh rupees as dowry or agree to *satta-batta*.

The *satta-batta* system of marriage is quite common in Punjab in which the bride's brother has to marry the groom's sister. So the deal was that I get married to Kamalpreet and become a US citizen. I get my family including my brother to the US and then my brother marries his maternal uncle's daughter and their uncle's family also settles there.

My parents were agreeable but when they learnt that the girl in question was handicapped, my brother backed out. People are so selfish nowadays...am so disappointed...Everything is business for them.

Thank God, I am still in touch with Gurjot. Did I mention him the last time? I guess no... He is the 'other' guy from Melbourne... He is ok...sweet...good looking but doesn't talk much. I have spoken to his folks more than I have spoken to him.

He is coming down to India early next month with his family. They say it's almost final from their side. They will take just a day to confirm it. Let's see...Beggars can't be choosers, as my mom says.

Chalo...will catcha later l guess...

Love,

P. Dhaliwal...

20th July 2012. 2355hrs.

≈

Hi Diary...

Gurjot had come to my house today with his parents. He is damnnnn good looking. He looks like that Punjabi singer Gary

Sandhu. Tall and handsome. And his surname is Sandhu too!

Well, he hardly talks, he looks pretty shy...but that can be changed, right?..:)

They confirmed the marriage and want us to do all the arrangements and suggest a date within the next three weeks. Oh! I am so excited!

Since this is an off season for weddings in Punjab, we will get the marriage hall booking easily. God! There is so much to do. Shopping for my wedding lehenga, buying jewellery, invitation cards...

I better rush now. Will catcha soon..

Lots of loveeeeee,

P. Dhaliwal

10th August 2012. 2030hrs.

≈

It has been two years since Sukhmanpreet got married. She got a job as a nurse within a month of landing in Australia and is getting a decent salary.

Gurjot is a nice guy but a little short tempered. He loses his temper at the drop of a hat. His mother is nice too and doesn't interfere much. On the surface, life seems smooth but something's seriously amiss.

After her marriage, there were some changes in the visa rules, and so Sukhmanpreet's parents are still in India. And she has also not been able to go to India.

She misses her family every single day. Today she's feeling especially low. Gurjot is out for somebody's wedding and would return late in the night.

She goes to the attic and opens her bag to have a look at her old pictures. As she looks at her family's pictures, her eyes became moist yet again. Her mom had made a copy of all the family albums and given it to her after her wedding.

Suddenly, at the bottom of her bag, she finds her old diary. She opens it and starts reading it.

Ah! I don't believe it! I was so desperate to come here. And look at me now. I so long to go back. Gosh! I am such an idiot.

She picks up a pen and starts writing.

~

Hi Diary,

It has been such a long, long time. I am Sukhmanpreet Kaur Sandhu now. The wedding was great. All of us had good fun. Most of my friends were able to make it to the wedding functions. I wore a magenta coloured lehenga. Everybody said I was looking very pretty. The pictures have come out well too.

What else! Life is okay otherwise. We bought a house last year. So busy making as much money as we can. I haven't met my parents in the last two years. I miss them so much! Gurjot says we can't afford to go right now because of the home loan liability and that we will go next year. I am keeping my fingers crossed. Let's see what happens.

Life is hectic here. I work night shifts at the hospital. Gurjot works day shifts. We meet for a little less than an hour each day. I have to cook and do the household chores myself. The whole concept of having servants for doing all the cooking and cleaning doesn't apply here, unlike in India.

Melbourne is beautiful. But I haven't made too many friends. People are a little cold, especially towards migrants. I experience a lot of racism here on a day-to-day basis though most of the Indians deny it. My husband doesn't have too many friends. Just a couple of Punjabi guys whom he used to stay with when he first came here. He works at a local restaurant as the head cook. His family had mentioned in his bio data that he was a restaurant manager. Anyway that's ok I guess. People do exaggerate. At the end of the day, a job is a job.

I think about Yashvir often. I wonder if he ever thinks about me.

So, ya, in all, life is not bad. But there's something amiss. Love, I guess. But, such is life.

Somebody so rightly said, 'Memories warm you up from the inside, but they also tear you apart.'

Love,

P. Dhaliwal

12th September 2014. 1530hrs.

A Murder in the Campus

Chandigarh, located near the foothills of the Himalayas, is known for its cleanliness and high per capita income. It is a planned city which serves as the capital of both Punjab and Haryana and is home to one of the oldest universities in India, Panjab University.

Panjab University (commonly referred to as PU or simply University by the locals) is notorious for its politicized student organizations, popularly known as PUSU (Panjab University Student's Union) and SOPU (Student Organization of Panjab University).

It is a common sight to see boys riding fancy motorcycles in groups and girls frolicking around in fashionable clothes around the university. PU students are also known for their high 'style' and 'political' quotient.

It is September and the university is gripped by 'Election Fever'. Different student parties have erected their tents on the campus and posted stickers with pictures of their candidates on tree trunks, electric poles, walls, vehicles and just about everywhere.

Candidates are leaving no stone unturned to ensure that they emerge victorious. Authorities have converted the university into a fort as the university elections are infamous for violence. The Dean, Mr. Verma, has been given a list of possible suspects who may try to create trouble.

Mr. Verma doesn't want to take a chance this time. Last year, a notorious member of a student party was shot at in broad daylight in the middle of the campus during campaigning. The boy survived after multiple operations and the case was closed citing lack of witnesses. Sneaking pistols, drugs and alcohol into the campus is common during the election time when votes are bought in lieu of alcohol and drugs.

~

Barely a week before the elections, the headline in the morning newspaper leaves everyone shocked.

PU STUDENT SHOT DEAD BY UNIDENTIFIED PERSONS

Chandigarh: A 19 year old student of the Panjab University was fatally shot outside the popular Club Elysium in Sector 17, though the exact circumstanes of the shooting are not yet clear. The victim has been identified as Zeeshan Singla, a 2nd year university student.

He was immediately taken to the nearest PGI hospital where he was pronounced dead.

Another unidentified woman, around 25 years of age was found unconscious with a wound on her head. Police say they are yet to identify any suspects.

More than 200 people were gathered inside the Club when the shooting occurred. Eye witnesses have told us that the two victims were found hand in hand at the spot when the police arrived hinting at a possible love angle. Sub Inspector SP Mehra told reporters that police was called to the site around midnight on Sunday. At the scene they found a male and a female victim lying in a pool of blood in the parking lot.

'It is believed that he was here at this location attending a party with a couple of his friends,' Mehra added.

The boy in question, Zeeshan, was a second year student of the University; an NRI who had come to Chandigarh for higher education. His family had shifted to Portland in the United States when he was five years old. His father and his local guardian were informed of his death last night.

The girl was still unidentified. Her photo was to appear in the next day's newspaper in an attempt to identify her.

After initial rounds of investigations, there were three theories doing the rounds in the police circles:

One, the two were lovers and were killed by a family member of the girl who probably opposed their affair; an honour killing scenario.

Two, it was a case of passion killing where the two lovers were killed by a third person; a love triangle scenario.

Three, the boy originally belonged to Ropar where a family dispute was underway between the boy's father and his paternal uncle. Hence the killing was over some disputed property, it is believed.

With each passing day the media coverage became louder and shriller.

By the third day, the news had created enough buzz in the city with increasing pressure on the police from the state government to close this case. The Chandigarh Inspector General, PS Goyal, assigned one of his most decorated investigation officers, DSP Sartaj Singh Dhindsa on this case who had recently been transferred to Chandigarh after a very successful stint in Amritsar.

DSP Dhindsa was known to be a no-nonsense cop who kept to himself. Apparently, his colleagues and friends made fun of him for being a tech freak behind his back. A lot of Rajnikant style jokes about him were doing the rounds in Chandigarh police circle. But he was totally unaware of this as no one dared to say anything in front of him.

Without wasting any time, Dhindsa reached Club Elysium within minutes of being assigned this case. A six-member police team followed him, waiting for further orders from him. At the cordoned-off site, his team started collecting whatever seemed relevant to the case although a team from the nearby local police station had already scanned the spot for clues the very first morning.

A total of three items were collected by the police team from the spot earlier in the day: a ladies handbag, a mini diary and a bike key.

The ladies handbag contained some cosmetics and currency notes. There was no identity proof in it. There was a mobile phone case but no mobile phone. The mini diary was full of poetry. It appeared to belong to the deceased boy. The key was sent for identification. Nothing seemed particularly relevant as of now.

Dhindsa removed his Nokia N97 smartphone, flipped it open and started typing a few entries.

He preferred his four year old smartphone with a keypad to the touch-based smartphones in the market today. What the hell is wrong with all the handset companies, he would often wonder! Why on earth would they think that everybody on this planet wants to use only the touch based phones. People like him and his wife hate these new touch based phones. Of course, his kids love them. But, they are so bloody inconvenient!

He made the following entries under a heading 'Top Qs - Elysium' in the Notes section:

> Who is the girl? Just a casual bystander or part of the whole fiasco?
> Was it a pre-planned or heat-of-the-moment attack?
> If pre-planned, what were the circumstances leading to the attack?

He then opened the To-Do app and started typing in the following entries:

Take handover from the local police station team

Visit the boy's college

Go through the contents of the diary personally

Visit the girl in the hospital

Take a follow up with Inspector Matharoo and the forensic team

The university students and the management were expecting a steady inflow of policemen and other investigating agencies for the next couple of days or at least, till the time the case was either solved or closed. Two separate police teams had already visited the campus since the incident happened. Dhindsa's was the third one.

The mood was gloomy and the weather, gloomier. It was autumn and the autumn mood seemed to be in sync with the mood at the university. So melancholic! The warmth of summer was suddenly gone, and the chill of winter was on the horizon. Skies turned grey, and the students at the university seemed to turn inward.

Today, the campus did not seem to be the same campus as it used to be. For the first time in its history, it was quiet. The management was yet to announce a decision on the imminent elections. There was uncertainty and fear in the air. One of the students had been killed and that too in such a brutal manner. Speculations were rife. Arguments were varied.

Dhindsa went straight to room number 109 of the Lala Lajpat Rai hostel, which was Zeeshan's room. His room partner was one Sarabjot Singh, a studious looking youth with high grades.

Dhindsa had pictured him in his head as a short boy with big spectacles. On the contrary, he turned out to be 6'4" tall, wearing a white kurta pyjama and a perfectly tied maroon coloured turban.

Oh, okay thought Dhindsa and smiled sheepishly when he saw Sarabjot.

A *hawaldar* accompanying him quickly brought a chair from another room. Dhindsa put his right foot on the chair instead of sitting on it. In no time, at least eight to ten other people filled the small hostel room.

"Sarabjot, I am going to be here for the next twenty minutes. I want you to tell me everything about your roommate Zeeshan. Girlfriends, enemies, friends etc. Everything. My questions will be short and your answers have to be long. Stop only when I tell you to. Is that clear? Yes or no?" Dhindsa spoke in a gruff voice, without mincing any words.

"Yes, sir."

"What kind of a boy was Zeeshan?"

"Sir, he was a quiet boy. He did not talk much and liked to spend most of his spare time writing or watching American television shows on his laptop...like Prison Break, How I Met Your Mother, Grey's Anatomy, Mad M..."

"Ok...ok...understood. what else?"

"He used to write a lot of stuff in his diary. You can go through the contents yourself. Maybe you will find a clue. He used to keep it locked in his almirah. Your guys broke open the lock in the morning and took it out."

A *hawaldar* handed over a maroon diary to Dhindsa as Sarabjot spoke.

"Hmm. So he was a quiet guy. So his friends were also like him?"

"Actually...sir...no...they weren't."

"His cousin Vikrant was vice president of PUSU two years ago. He passed out from the university last year. Plus Zeeshan was an NRI. So you know how it is here. He didn't have to try hard to fit anywhere...a lot of people wanted to be friends with him and include him in their group."

"So. What's your point?" Dhindsa said curtly.

"Actually he was a part of a notorious group called Knight Riders. So maybe it was a group rivalry thing, Red Bulls and Knight Riders would often lock horns inside and outside the campus. So maybe."

"Knight Riders! Red Bulls!..Hah!" Dhindsa smirked and said in a mocking manner.

"Sir! There are around ten odd gangs in PU...but there are two such gangs which are very prominent and everyone in the University is scared of them."

"O really!...Why is everybody scared of them? What do they do?" he added sarcastically.

"Sir, there is fierce rivalry between these two groups. Over elections, girls, hangouts, *gedi* routes. They leave no opportunity to pounce at each other."

Gedi routes are designated routes where boys drive around on their bikes while the girls, dressed in all their finery, just hang around and try to get maximum attention from the boys.

"I see."

"Zeeshan would often tell me that he would do anything for his group if the need arose...his parents are separated and his friends were his biggest support. He was an extremely emotional guy."

"Even last year's shooting at the campus was speculated to be the handiwork of one of these gangs."

Sarabjot then went on to name a few prominent gang members of both the gangs. Dhindsa started noting the same in his phone though one of his team members was recording the conversation anyway.

"Hmm. Did he have any girlfriend?"

"Yes sir, but they broke up last month."

"Is this the one?" Dhindsa showed him the picture of the girl in coma.

"No sir, I have never seen this girl with Zeeshan or otherwise in the campus ever."

"Hmm...Ok...I will go through his diary and will let you know if I need any more information from you."

"Yes...sir...sure."

Dhindsa came out of the hostel and proceeded towards the

police station for a meeting. After a long meeting with his team members who had gathered a lot of information from the CCTV footage and eye witness accounts, he listed the following names on a white board:

Gang 1 - Red Bulls

Arshjot Singh Parmar : Age 20. Son of a prominent city builder Kishan Singh Parmar. Motherless. Spoilt brat. Arrogant.

Navtej Singh Deol : Age 22. Belongs to a well-connected political Deol family. Immature. Over-confident. Hot-headed.

Iqbal Singh Kamboj : Age 22. Rich farmer's only son. Intelligent. Opportunist. Womanizer.

Gururaj Singh Chahal : Age 21. Great grandson of an erstwhile Maharaja. Polished. Dominating. Music lover.

Gang 2 - Knight Riders

Arjun Khanna : Age 23. Son of civil servants. Movie star looks. Biker. Narcissist.

Zeeshan Singla : Age 19. NRI. Product of a broken home. Confused soul. Loner. Poet.

Sanjeet Singh Saini : Age 20. Son of a cloth merchant. Ambitious. Funny.

Rajbir Mallik : Age 20. Son of a property broker. Drug addict. Dreamer.

From the CCTV footage of the Club Elysium, Dhindsa could

confirm the presence of four people from the list. Zeeshan and Arjun were present with four other boys while Iqbal and Arshjot were the only ones from the other group. The girl was present in the party but was not a part of either of these two groups. She could be seen drinking alone at the bar in the CCTV footage.

Dhindsa instructed his team member Inspector Matharoo to get seven arrest warrants issued against the gang members. He wanted them in police custody as soon as possible. Since all of the seven in question were from influential families, they tried to exert varying degrees of influence on the investigations. Dhindsa was flooded with calls in the next couple of hours from ministers to bureaucrats. But Dhindsa stood firm, not giving in to any pressure.

Arshjot, Navtej and Arjun were the most difficult to catch hold of. Almost all of them were huddled up in secret locations, distant relatives' houses, hotels and farm houses. The police tracked phone calls, interrogated family members and the domestic help to locate the boys.

Dhindsa was fortunate as he could get hold of the boys but only due to the national media exposure that this case was under, otherwise it would have been impossible.

All seven boys are brought to the interrogation room one by one. Dhindsa wanted to interrogate them all by himself. He just keeps one *hawaldar* with him to coordinate the interrogation.

The policemen at the station were busy discussing the case.

Policeman 1 : It is crystal clear...it is a case of gang rivalry.

Policeman 2 : Yes...Yes clearly...one of those Red Bulls guy shot him in anger or something.

Policeman 1 : Red Bulls! Knight Riders! What nonsense!

Policeman 2 : All rich kids...they have to do something for entertainment, right?

Policeman 1 : All seven kids are from rich families...no point wasting time on this...soon a couple of telephone calls and these kids will drive away in their fancy cars.

Policeman 2 : Obviously!

The first boy to be called inside the interrogation room is Gururaj, a tall and well built turbaned boy wearing a collared T-shirt with cotton pants. He looks every bit a prince in his manner and gait.

Gururaj : Sir, please listen to me, I am innocent.

Dhindsa : And why should I believe you, young man?

Gururaj : Sir, I was in my hostel canteen when they were partying.

Dhindsa: Are you sure?

Gururaj : Sir, you may ask anybody in the campus.

Dhindsa turning towards *hawaldar* waiting at the door. *Hawaldar* Yadav, take him to the other room. Send the next boy in.

Gururaj : Thank you sir. Thank you.

Sanjeet enters the room.

He is around 5'8" tall, potbellied, wearing a funny looking yellow cap and resembles a cartoon character. Sanjeet : Sir, I swear I have no clue...am innocent...please believe me.

Dhindsa : Tell me what I want to hear buddy.

Sanjeet : Sir, I was sleeping in my room when they left for the club. I did not feel like going. You can ask my roommate if you wish.

Dhindsa : That I will. Or probably I already would have asked, you worry about your skin, boy...anything else you want to tell me?

Sanjeet : Hmm...no sir...that is it sir.

Dhindsa : Yadav! Get the next boy in...you can go, boy and wait in the next room.

Sanjeet : Sir, anybody from our group will have no reason to kill him. He was our friend.

Dhindsa : Hmmm...ok...I see.

Navtej enters next. He looks like a typical overgrown kid. Smart but cocky. Arrogant and disrespectful. He has been involved in at least five earlier cases, so he appears a lot calmer compared to the others. Belonging to a well known political family also helps.

Navtej clearly is in no mood to claim that he is innocent or justify anything. Dhindsa doesn't talk but just stares at him for a good long ten minutes.

Finally, he opens his mouth to speak.

Dhindsa : Yes, boy. So why did you shoot the opposite gang member?

Navtej : I am not a fool to shoot him in a public place.

Dhindsa : Then who killed him?

Navtej : I have no clue.

Dhindsa : Did you go there to party that evening?

Navtej : No. You can check the CCTV footage.

Dhindsa : That I will. Did you go there after the party was over?

Navtej : Yes. I did.

Dhindsa : Why?

Navtej : Arshjot had called me.

Dhindsa : Keep talking.

Navtej : They got into a fight with Knight Riders.

Dhindsa : So you went there and killed Zeeshan in anger?

Navtej : Why would I kill Zeeshan? Why would anybody kill Zeeshan? I would rather kill somebody else..Hah! He was a harmless guy. We had no issues with him ever. Ask anybody.

Dhindsa : What did you do when you went there?

Navtej : What was to be done? We had an altercation with the Knight Riders after which we left.

Dhindsa : Altercation! Physical or verbal?

Navtej : Physical.

Dhindsa : Who was carrying a pistol?

Navtej, wiping his face with a handkerchief : Nobody was.

Dhindsa : Ok...So you don't want to talk! I see. Wait outside and I will come back to you again.

Navtej : As you wish.

Navtej gets up and leaves the room and Rajbir is called in next.

Rajbir Mallik looks totally sloshed even now. He can't walk or talk straight. He look twenty years older than his age with sagging skin and bloodshot eyes.

Dhindsa : Do you want to say anything...?

Rajbir : N. Noo...I don't k...know anything...sssir.

Dhindsa : Where were you when this happened?

Rajbir : Sir...I already ttoldd the p.p.police...was watching a mmmovie...

Dhindsa : Which movie?

Rajbir : *Go Goa Gone.*

Dhindsa : Where?

Rajbir : Sir...Fun Cinemas...

Dhindsa : You mean Sector 17 Fun Cinemas?

Rajbir : Yyesss...Ssirr...

Dhindsa : How was the movie?

Rajbir : G...g...good.

Dhindsa : Ok...am done...go to the room this side (he said pointing towards the room on the right)...Yadav! next.

Arjun enters the room, looking around like a lost puppy. Tall, fair and lean, Arjun has the looks of a movie star but right now he looks shattered. With his puffy eyes and uncombed hair it seems he has not slept for days.

Dhindsa : How was the party that day?

Arjun : Sir?

Dhindsa : I asked how the party was that day.

Arjun : Okay, sir.

Dhindsa : Just ok? The videos show something else. You were the star of the evening.

Arjun : No. Sir.

Dhindsa : Modest boy. Hmmm...I am sure you weren't this modest that day. I read about this German saying online, 'Where wine goes in, modesty goes out.' What happened that night? Tell me everything...I think you got too drunk and shot your friend. Is that right?

Arjun : No sir. No sir. I swear...I didn't.

Dhindsa : All evidence points towards you as of now. Red Bulls gang people left before you. Your four friends left after them and you two were the only ones to leave in the end. All sloshed, huh?

Arjun : No sir. There was a fight after the party. In the parking lot. I will tell you everything...everything...

Dhindsa asks for a glass of water to be given to Arjun who is sweating profusely. He gulps down the water hurriedly and composes himself.

Arjun : Sir, Zeeshan and I were the last ones to come out of the party. The club was closed half an hour before that and we were whisked out from the back door. When we came out, we were surprised to see my bike badly damaged. It appeared as if somebody had smashed it with something.

We turned around to see Arshjot and Iqbal standing with hockey sticks. Before we could realize what was happening, they started beating us. The girl how is in the hospital now started yelling. A few people came to our rescue. Zeeshan and I picked up some stones and started throwing at them.

Dhindsa : Ok...then. Who shot whom?

Arjun : I don't know sir. All I know is that Zeeshan called up Sanjeet who came down within no time. A few minutes after Sanjeet came Gururaj, Navtej and Rajbir also arrived. There was chaos all around and suddenly I heard gun shots...and before I could realize what is happening, I saw Zeeshan slump down on the ground. He was bleeding. Everybody except Rajbir and Sanjeet fled the scene...I...I tried to call the ambulance but nobody picked up the call. Zeeshan had stopped breathing. I was too scared. So I ran away.

Dhindsa : Ok. So you don't know who shot Zeeshan. And what about the girl?

Arjun : I don't know about her sir. She was just crying and yelling at everybody to stop. She kept on saying, "I will call the police..." but...but...I saw Iqbal trying to shut her up and was gagging her with his hands.

Dhindsa : Ok...I see...go wait outside, I will get back to you.

Arjun : Yes Sir. Please...am innocent...I didn't do anything. Please help me. My career will be ruined.

Dhindsa : Your friend is dead and one innocent girl is battling for her life. Go and sit outside quietly. And try to recall anything else if you can. It will only help me help you. Yadav...call the remaining two boys together.

It is 8 p.m. and it is dark outside.

Arshjot and Iqbal enter the room.

Dhindsa : You two were all over the place that night. The CCTV cameras have captured you drinking like there's no tomorrow. And you were seen leaving the club with the girl. Now, if you two want to save your skin, blurt out everything quickly. Who was the girl? What does she have to do with Zeeshan?

Arshjot is breathing heavily and looks really scared. He is trembling with fear. From his body language, it seems that he knows what happened.

Iqbal looks at Arshjot and neither of them utter a word. Dhindsa gets up and fetches a glass of water for Arshjot. Arshjot picks up the glass and gulps the water down.

Dhindsa : Do you want to talk now? Does the weapon belong to you?

Arshjot : Sir, I stole that pistol from my father's room a day before the incident. I just wanted to show it around in the campus. When the fight got out of hand, I took out the pistol that was kept in my car and fired twice in the air. Out of nowhere, Rajbir pounced on me. I fell down and a fistfight ensued. He threw sand in my eyes and managed to snatch my pistol. Sir...I swear. I don't know what happened after that...when I opened my eyes I saw Zeeshan lying on the ground and this girl yelling her lungs out.

Dhindsa : Iqbal, what did you see?

Iqbal : I don't know. I didn't see anything...Rajbir must have shot Zeeshan.

Dhindsa : Why would Raj...?

Before Dhindsa is able to complete his question, an officer comes inside and asks Dhindsa to accompany him to the IG's office. Dhindsa nods and the officer leaves the room and Dhindsa turns back to Iqbal.

Dhindsa : Why would Rajbir shoot Zeeshan?

Iqbal : Sir, most of us were drunk but Rajbir seemed to be under the influence of some heavy-duty drugs…he is a drug addict… everybody in the campus knows that.

Arshjot : Sir, I think he was trying to shoot Navtej who was hitting Zeeshan but by mistake shot Zeeshan.

Dhindsa's mobile is continuously ringing. He looks at his mobile. He knows he needs to take the call but wants to get all the information before that.

Dhindsa : What about the girl? Who was she and who struck her?

Iqbal : Sir. The girl was not known to us, I approached her near the washrooms and invited her to join us. And she agreed.

Arshjot : Sir, she appeared to be a call girl or something.

Dhindsa : Who knocked her unconscious?

Iqbal : I…I…don't know sir. We have told you what we saw.

Dhindsa : Are you sure, Iqbal?

Iqbal : Y…yes…Sir…

Hawaldar Yadav comes in and tells Dhindsa that there is a big chaos outside and there are orders from the seniors to stop the interrogation immediately. Dhindsa dismisses him with a wave of his hand.

Dhindsa : Where is the pistol?

Arshjot : Sir, don't know, I think Rajbir threw it or something. We don't know.

Dhindsa : I see...even if I believe you for a minute. Do you know that since the bullet was fired from the pistol carried by you to the scene of crime, you will be found guilty of murder unless some witness comes forward and proves otherwise?

Arshjot breaks down when he hears this.

Dhindsa : Listen to me carefully now, if you want me to save your ass, tell me truthfully what happened to the girl.

Arshjot : Sir, sir...I will tell you everything. When I opened my eyes, I saw Zeeshan on the ground and the pistol lying next to him. I panicked and quickly picked up the pistol. I was scared that I would be blamed for the murder.

Dhindsa : Why did you hurt the girl?

Iqbal : Sir, she was yelling that she will report us to the police. I panicked, snatched the pistol from Arsh's hands and hit her on the head with the pistol. Sir...I swear I didn't want to hurt her.

Dhindsa : Where is the pistol?

Arshjot : Sir, we threw it in a village pond on our way back to Iqbal's house.

IGP PS Goyal marches inside the room with an angry scowl on his face.

Goyal : What the hell, Dhindsa? I told you to report to me immediately!

Dhindsa is startled but he stands up and salutes his senior.

Dhindsa : I have almost cracked the case, Sir.

Goyal : I don't care, Dhindsa. Come with me quickly.

As Dhindsa steps out, he sees a barrage of media persons, lawyers and family members at the gate. Goyal takes him to his room and switches on the TV.

"Breaking News. University murder case solved!"

A news reader was hurriedly giving details on the case:

"A man named Sushant Sharma surrendered himself in the Chandigarh murder case. He has been identified as the long time personal assistant of eminent businessman Mr. K S Parmar. Sushant is believed to be very close to Mr. Parmar's son Arshjot, who was part of the brawl outside the club. According to the reports, the pistol used in the murder was registered in the name of Mr. Parmar. It was a licensed pistol. According to our sources, Sushant stole Mr. Parmar's pistol from his bedroom drawer early in the evening. He was reported to be drunk that evening and was present on the spot when the incident happened. He is believed to have shot two rounds in the air and then fired one shot at Zeeshan Singla, killing him immediately. He then hit the girl on her head in a bid to silence her. It is not yet clear what was Sushant doing outside Club Elysium at that time. Was he called by Arshjot or one of his friends? We will be answering all these questions after this short break. Be with us!"

Goyal switches on another channel. Mr. K S Parmar was seen

holding a press conference and blaming the police for harassing his son unnecessarily.

He can be heard saying, "Is this what I get for being an eminent businessman. My son is an innocent student who had gone to that place to relax with his friends. The real culprit has already surrendered to the police an hour ago. The police are dragging my innocent son into this matter without even verifying the facts. If this is not harassment, then what is?"

~

Arjun and Zeeshan arrive at around 8 pm with four other friends on their bikes...they park their three bikes together.

Iqbal arrives with Arshjot in a BMW car. An hour later they misbehave with a group of girls on their way in. The club manager tries his best to tell them not to create trouble.

They party for more than two hours.

Arjun comes out for a smoke with a friend of his, and on seeing Arshjot's BMW takes a stone and smashes his side door glass with it. Just for fun…

The party is almost over at around midnight and most of the party goers leave. Iqbal and Arshjot also come out. Iqbal has picked up a call girl on his way out and both of them are totally sloshed. The girl starts screaming.

On seeing his damaged car. Arshjot flies into a rage. He had already located Zeeshan and Arjun in the club earlier.

He enters the two wheeler parking lot and starts kicking Arjun's bike. Arjun and Zeeshan come out with their friends...and on seeing Arshjot damaging Arjun's bike, a fight erupts...one of their friends calls Rajbir and Sanjeet.

Meanwhile Arshjot calls Gururaj and Navtej to the spot.

Arshjot whips out his pistol and tries to scare the other gang. Arjun knocks him over with a punch. The gun falls down and Rajbir picks it up. He has been smoking up in his room and had come there in a trance. He picks up the gun and shoots at the opposite group in the heat of the moment. The bullet hits Zeeshan and he falls in a heap on the ground. The girl starts screaming. Iqbal hits her on the head with a bottle in the melee and both fall down. The Red Bulls gang flees from the scene.

Arjun and Sanjeet drag Rajbir away from the scene.

Zeeshan is dead.

The girl's screams slowly die out.

The Miracle Maharaj

It is 7 am.

The stage is set.

The flower-decked throne is ready.

Everybody is waiting for HIM to arrive.

A huge *pandal* is set up in the ashram grounds, ten kilometres outside Ambala city. More than ten thousand followers comprising of men, women as well as children from all over Punjab have assembled for the *satsang* today. Five hundred volunteers dressed in white kurta pyjamas are struggling to manage the crowds and get everybody seated. Women and children are seated on the right side while the men are seated on the left. The stage is decorated with expensive flowers. The holy seat where HE will sit is made of gold, or at least it looks like that. Air conditioners are installed in the area near the stage while the rest of the *pandal* has fans hanging from the ceiling. Water dispensers are installed at various points outside the *pandal*.

Giant screens are set up on either side of the stage, the floor of which is made up of black glass. There is an area for *yagna* in front of the stage. Songs praising HIM are playing at full volume on speakers installed inside and outside the *pandal*. The followers know the songs by heart and are singing along in unison.

It is a very hot day and inside the *pandal* it feels like one is in a furnace. Hundreds of hand-fans can be seen in the hands of the followers. People are still waiting in long queues to get in. The venue appears more than full and there is no chance that they can be accommodated inside. Those already in the *pandal* had stood in queue since the previous night to get in.

Eight year old Chinki, sitting somewhere in the middle of the right row, is straining her neck every now and then to see if HE has arrived. Chinki has come with her mother Gurdeep Kohli from Pabri village near Rajpura in Punjab. They took a bus from their village to Rajpura from where they took a train to Ambala. Gurdeep, a primary school teacher at the government school in Pabri is HIS loyal follower and does not miss any of HIS *satsangs*.

Finally at 7.45 am, HE arrives in all HIS splendour.

Welcome music!

Loud chants!

Flower shower!

Theatrical fog!

Orange robe!

Turban adorned with jewels!

Param Pujya Chamatkari Baba Maharaj Jaidev ji takes his seat. He appears to be around sixty years of age. He is a tall man with a long white beard and long hair which is tied at the back of his head with an orange band. He holds up both his hands and with a beatific smile on his face, looks from right to left acknowledging the presence of the people in the *pandal*.

The followers are brimming with excitement. The chants become louder and louder. The women, especially the ones sitting in the front, are swaying while chanting his name.

Two women faint on seeing Maharaj ji and are helped by paramedics available at the spot.

Maharaj ji gestures to the crowd to calm down. Two men wearing long white robes take their place on either side of his throne. They are bald and are not wearing turbans.

Chinki is watching him as if mesmerised. No prizes for guessing that this is a first of its kind event for her.

As she had waited in the queue to enter the *pandal*, she had overheard two ladies speaking about Maharaj ji possessing some supernatural powers and performing miracles. She is now looking forward to some magic tricks, but is surprised when instead the discourse starts.

Chinki pulls her mother's dupatta to grab her attention, as she seems to be in a trance.

'What is the matter?' asks Gurdeep in an irritated tone.

Gurdeep was forced to get Chinki along with her as there was no one at home to look after her. Till two months ago, when her mother-in-law was alive, Gurdeep would leave Chinki in her care.

Chinki's father had died four years ago in a train accident near Ludhiana. A few months after her husband's death, Gurdeep was introduced to Maharaj ji by her neighbour Dhani Ram's mother, who was known as Badi Bibi in the neighbourhood. Badi Bibi claimed that Dhani Ram had 'died' of a snake bite when he was a teenager and she took his 'body' to Maharaj ji, at the suggestion of the village sarpanch. Maharaj ji sprinkled some holy ash on her dead son and told her to leave him in the room and wait outside.

"I was going mad and had given up any hope of getting my son back. But, what do I see? After an hour the door in front of me opened and my son walked out wearing a white robe," Badi Bibi said in an exaggerated tone. Gurdeep believed every word she said.

"Veer ji was reborn?" asked Gurdeep, referring to Dhani Ram as Veer ji, as is usually the norm in the village. All men of or close to one's age are referred to as Veer ji, meaning brother.

So impressed was Gurdeep by this miraculous story that she decided to follow Maharaj ji and started believing that only he could get her life back on track. She never missed any of his events, no matter which part of the country it was being held in. She was at risk of losing her teaching job since she had taken leaves far in excess of the permitted number.

"Mummy, when will the magic show start?"

"Shhhhhhh.....Lower your voice. And magic show! What magic show? Who the hell told you that?"

"Those ladies in the queue were saying th..."

"This is not a magic show, you stupid disrespectful girl. Just keep quiet and sit still," said Gurdeep before turning away.

Chinki felt very disappointed as she had been quite excited at the prospect of watching a magic show. She is feeling very hungry. The plastic box containing biscuits is kept safely in a green cloth bag, tucked under her mother's left thigh. She is scared at the thought of disturbing her mother again. She doesn't want to get slapped like last week, when she was pestering her mother in the Gurudwara about the delay in the start of *langar*, a communal meal for all.

She is bored and restless and tries to while away time by playing with her silver anklets.

She is missing her grandmother today.

Maharaj ji is speaking about his dream in which God appeared and gave him divine powers. His voice is silvery. He says that right now, God is speaking through him. It seems only the voice is his; the words are coming from a bigger source.

Another hour has passed.

No magic show yet.

Chinki gets up with a sudden jerk. She looks angry and starts walking towards the nearest exit. One of the volunteers notices her but thinks she is going out to have water from the dispenser installed next to the nearest gate. As she takes a couple of steps from her seat, her anger turns into fear as she notices the number of people in the *pandal*. She has never seen so many people together at one place. She contemplates going back but decides to proceed ahead, as she is feeling anxious and suffocated.

After a few minutes of manoeuvring through the crowd, she manages to come out.

There is a lot of dust outside. She covers her face with her dupatta. She does not want another episode of asthma, like the one that happened last month. She locates a water dispenser a few steps away from the exit. She is feeling very thirsty and walks towards it.

There are no cups or glasses near the dispenser. She cups her left hand and bends down to drink water. She presses the knob of the plastic tap with her right hand, but nothing happens.

She is feeling very frustrated and on the verge of tears. She is frantically pressing the knob and tilting the dispenser to get some water out of it. She looks around to see if anybody is around. Finally, she notices a volunteer coming out from another exit gate, a little distance away from where she is standing.

She tries to get his attention.

"Bhaiiyaaa"

"Bhaiiyaaaaaa"

"Aye Bhaiiyaaa..."

"Sunooooo..."

The loudspeakers are on full volume. Maharaj ji's voice is the only thing that can be heard.

Maharaj ji is now speaking about the cosmic truths about death, the hidden secrets of birth and the inner awakening.

The volunteer looks towards the other side, as if trying to locate something and goes back inside. Clearly, he did not hear her desperate cries.

After struggling for another few minutes, she realizes that there is no water in the dispenser. She starts moving towards another dispenser that she can see at a distance.

She is less than a metre away from the dispenser when she faints.

~

When she opens her eyes, she finds herself in a room full of onions and potatoes. She looks around and notices a pot full of water in one corner of the room. She gets up, picks up a glass lying next to the pot and drinks some water.

This room seems to be somewhere behind the stage as Maharaj ji's voice can be heard at a distance. She feels relieved to know that she is still somewhere near the *pandal*.

She hears the sound of footsteps from outside the door and before she can find a place to hide, the door opens and a man dressed in a long white robe, similar to the ones worn by the men sitting next to Maharaj ji, enters the room. He has shaggy brown hair and a toothy smile.

She sits crouched near a big bag of onions.

"*Kaaki*, are you ok now?" the man asks. His smile scares her.

As she raises her head, she blows out a slow breath.

"Where is my mummy?"

"Oh! I thought you will know! We were going to ask you." He looks mighty pleased as he says this.

"I want to go to my mummy."

"Why *kaaki*? Be with us here at Maharaj ji's ashram?" he says again in a very sarcastic tone.

"No...no...no...Please...I want to go home."

"Ok...Ok...Let the event get over, then we will make an announcement on the stage."

"No...I can find my mummy on my own. Let me go."

"A lot of people who were waiting outside have come inside the *pandal*. It is very crowded now. You will not be able to find her. We will make an announcement on the stage. Don't worry. Ok?"

"*Haanji...Ok.*"

The man smiles again before going out. He leaves the door open. Chinki moves close to the door after he leaves.

She can hear him talking to someone else.

"Don't let the girl go out. We will keep her." She hears the man say in an undertone.

"Ok...guruji," says a woman with a husky voice.

We will keep her.

The line is echoing in Chinki's ears.

What do they mean, they will keep me? How can they keep me like that? I will shout and tell everybody. But, what if they do? Where will they take me?

She can feel tears rolling down her cheeks.

All of a sudden, she gets a sudden burst of energy. She wipes her tears with both her hands. She gathers courage and peeps outside the room from the front door. She can see a woman in a white salwar kameez with her back towards her speaking to a boy. The boy is not more than fifteen years old and is wearing a white kurta pyjama like the volunteers inside the *pandal*. He seems to be one of them.

The woman is heard telling him in hushed tones, "*Oye munde*, don't let the girl go out ok? I will be back in an hour. I need to oversee the new member induction process."

"Ok ji."

The woman turns towards the door. Chinki moves inside swiftly but is sure the woman is going to lock the door.

To her surprise, the woman just walks past the door without even peeping in. She seems to be in a hurry.

Chinki gets up and tries to find another door or an open window at the back of the room. Her mind is racing. She wants to get out of this place as soon as possible.

Just then she hears someone say, 'What happened? Are you hungry?'

The boy walks in.

"Y...y...yes..." This is all she manages to say.

"Hmmm...Ok...Wait for ten more minutes. I will get something for you after they take this machine out of the room," the boy says pointing towards a corner of the room.

Chinki turns around and sees something that she has not noticed in all the while she has been in this room. Hidden behind the stack of onions, she sees this machine that looks like a smaller version of a combine-harvester, which is used for harvesting grain crops in her village.

"Ok..." says Chinki matter-of-factly.

After about ten minutes, she hears a loud commotion. Six strongly built men walk into the room. They seem to be in a tearing hurry.

The boy takes Chinki by her arm and escorts her out of the room.

All of the men are speaking at once.

"Come on...be quick."

"...You hold it from the back..."

"...Fast...its starting in five minutes...the cue music has already started..hurry up."

Two men are frantically removing onions and potatoes from the way.

"...Hold it...hold it..."

"...Keep moving..."

It was a mini storm that lasted for not more than a few minutes, but left a lot of mess in the room. Chinki peeps back inside with wide eyes. There is no room for her to even stand there anymore.

"This always happens...You want to see Maharaj ji's *vibhuti* miracle." the boy asks trembling with apparent excitement. *Vibhuti* is the term used for sacred ash, usually white in colour. It is used for religious worship in India.

"*Vibhuti* miracle! What is that?...I don't want to see anything...I want to go back to my mummy."

"Oh...your mummy? She is here? See...all that I don't know...But I don't want to wait here and miss the miracle...I missed it the last time too..."

"No. Take me to my mummy please!" Chinki pleads with the boy, her eyes filling up with tears.

"Ok, let's make a deal. You come with me to see the miracle and then I will tell Gujji *mata* to take you to your mummy, ok?'

It seems Gujji *mata* is the woman with the husky voice.

"Ok," she agrees. Her brain is working well enough to know that this option is better than being stuck in a room full of onions and potatoes.

"Fine. Let's go. But promise me you will not tell Gujji *mata* that I took you there. Just say we were waiting right here all the time," the boy says innocently trying his best to strike a deal.

"Ok."

He holds her hand so as to ensure he doesn't lose her and starts walking towards the hallway. Chinki is looking around to figure out where she is.

Maharaj ji's voice becomes louder and clearer as they move forward. The hallway appears to be never-ending, till the boy drags her out, with a sudden jerk, from a small exit door on one side of the hallway.

"Ouuchhhh, *Bhaiyyyaa*... Where are we going?"

"Shhhhhh...To see the miracle from the best spot, you dumb girl...now keep quiet and just move."

Now, they are in the open. She can clearly see the *pandal* a little ahead from where they are standing. There is a giant marble statue of Maharaj ji mounted on a black stone platform, ahead of the *pandal*.

The sun is hot and bright which makes her feel giddy again. It seems they have been walking in the sun for a very long time. She can hear loud chants of people inside the *pandal*. It seems like the miracle is going to start any time soon.

The boy starts running and dragging her along, as he approaches the *pandal*.

"Fast...fast...you stupid girl...I don't want to miss it again."

To her surprise, he leads her to the statue, instead of moving straight, towards the *pandal*.

"Bhaiiyaa...where are you taking me?"

He doesn't respond and pulls her towards the tall back stone platform under the statue. He pulls a small knob that looks like a part of the engraving on the platform.

Chinki is standing there, transfixed, as a door opens and they walk in. She is taken aback at what she sees. They are in a dark underground passage.

She is so scared. It feels like a nightmare and she is desperately hoping that somebody will wake her up.

As they walk, the passage narrows down. They take a few steps and then the boy turns back and whispers, "Do not utter a single word now. Ok?"

She doesn't say anything.

"Follow me quietly," he tells her.

He leaves her hand and tiptoes forward. She follows him.

They are now directly under the black glass stage on which the Maharaj ji is seated. She can see the passage still going ahead right below the *yagna* area in front of the stage. There are a few wooden steps next to where she is standing. The boy moves sideways and climbs onto the steps stealthily. He looks down towards her and whispers, 'Aye *choti*...You want to see this?'

She is scared yet inquisitive. She climbs up the steps too. What she sees blows her mind. They are inside the black glass stage now and she can see the *yagna* area and the crowd seated right in front of her. It is clear that the crowd cannot see them, behind the glass, which seems to be a one-way tinted mirror.

She sees the vast crowd in front of her. The man with the crooked smile was right. There are more people in the *pandal* than she saw last. All the people in the queue outside are let in to witness the *vibhuti* miracle.

How will I find my mother in this crowd?

Will I ever meet my mother again?

What are these people going to do with me?

Do they know I am not in that room?

Have they already started searching for me?

Who is this boy?

Chinki is trying to locate her mother in the crowd.

"Woww...it has started...it has started. Now see how the crowd reacts," the boys whispers with palpable excitement.

A mini ash storm starts from the *yagna kund*. The chants grow louder and louder.

Chinki climbs down the steps. The boy's eyes are fixed on the scene in front of him. He does not notice her.

She takes a few steps towards the passage leading to the area under the *yagna kund* where the *vibhuti* storm is happening.

She sees the same six men operating the combine harvester type machine they took out from the room she was kept in. Two of them are putting sacks of some flour like thing into an opening of the machine, two are operating the machine and the remaining two are holding the machine down, as it vibrates vigorously.

She takes a turn and starts running towards the passage she has come from. She passes by the steps, on top of which the boy is enjoying the 'miracle'. Without another thought, she runs towards the exit.

It is taking her forever to reach there. She feels like she is running on the same spot. She looks back to see if anyone is following her.

There is nobody.

She reaches the door, opens the latch and runs outside. The chants are much louder here. She has no energy left in her and yet, she is running like a maniac towards the *pandal*.

~

Apparently, Maharaj ji has disappeared in the *vibhuti* storm.

The event is over and the awe-struck crowd is being instructed over the loud speakers to start dispersing.

Gurdeep comes out of her trance to find Chinki missing. She gets up and tries to push her way through the crowd, but it is virtually impossible. There is a sea of people around her. Her feet are getting trampled and her ribs are getting elbowed. She feels a sudden push from behind and falls down.

Nobody cares.

She lets out a shrill cry.

'Chinkiiiiiiiiiiiiiiiiiiiiiiiiiiiiiiiiiiiiii!'

The Five Metre Burden

1...2...3....

Yes...yes...

Now ...repeat...

Yes...

Very good...*Shabaash*...see...it's done.

So, there you go. Fourteen year old Kanwer Singh Cheema just learnt to tie his own turban.

~

Five years later

Kanwer comes out of his house, all dressed up and ready to go to college. He is pursuing a B.Com degree from the upscale Fergusson College in Pune. Fergusson College is known as much for the fashion quotient of its students as it is for its heritage building, like so many other colleges in Pune. A vibrant, booming metropolis, Pune is an educational, business and cultural hub that epitomises the 'New India'.

Kanwer is riding his two-stroke single-cylinder Yamaha RX 100, that he had purchased from a second hand motorcycle dealer last week. Though his cousin Surjeet from Amritsar advised him to go for the Royal Enfield Bullet 350 classic, he thought otherwise. He was in no mood to listen to Surjeet anyway, especially after he had advised him to buy a Bajaj Scooter and Kanwer had been stuck with the damn scooter for two years. Looking back, he felt that he made a complete fool of himself all through junior college.

He is smiling as he approaches the popular FC Road, named after his college. But just before entering FC Road he takes a turn and slows his bike to a halt in a narrow lane next to his college. Kanwer looks around nervously and using both his hands removes the turban from his head, presses it a little from both sides to flatten it and puts it in his backpack. He ruffles his newly cropped, short hair with his fingers and admires himself in the rear view mirror of his bike. Beaming with happiness, he turns back his bike towards his college.

He feels he resembles Hrithik Roshan, the Bollywood star from the recent hit movie, *Krish 2*. Just like the handsome actor, Kanwer too is light-eyed.

As he enters the college gate with a confident stride, he feels that everybody is looking at him.

~

There had been a big family scene at home last night. Kanwer had finally got his long hair cropped after his father, retired Brigadier DS Cheema, refused to grant him permission to do so, despite repeated attempts. To the best of his memory, Kanwer had been trying to convince his father for the last four years.

"Get out of my house!" thundered Brig. Cheema

"Please don't do that...I beg of you," pleaded Mrs. Cheema.

"You go to your room," he yelled at his wife, seething with anger, his face the colour of a tomato.

Kanwer stood there smirking with pride. In his head, he knew his father would not throw him out of the house. After all, he is their only son.

Mrs. Cheema started crying.

"How can you act like that? Look at what your son has done," an astonished Brig. Cheema asked his wife.

"I don't know...it is ok...I will tell him to grow his hair back," Mrs.Cheema entreated, sobbing quietly; her love for her son was greater than her love for her husband.

Silence.

The mother looked at her husband with pleading eyes.

The father took a step towards him, pointed his finger, and

opened his mouth to speak but before he could utter a word, a defiant Kanwer shot back. "No. I will not grow back my hair."

A long silence.

Tough looks and stares were exchanged between the father and the son, while the mother continued sobbing quietly in the background.

"What did you say?"

"I said I will NOT grow my hair back."

"And, why on earth is that?"

"Dad, are you really asking me why! Because I am tired of it. Because my head hurts every day. Because I feel different from the others."

"So, what is the problem in looking or feeling different from the others? Isn't that a good thing?"

"No, I don't want to look different."

"And what is this utter nonsense about the head hurting bit? Lakhs of Sikhs have long hair and tie a turban, nothing happens to them. Most of the women in India tie their hair a bun. Your head is made of glass or what?"

"I don't know. My head hurts and that's the truth."

"With the hair pulled up or with the turban?"

"How does that matter?"

"It does. Tell me. It hurts because of the hair pulled up or because of the turban?"

"Fine. I guess...w...w...with the hair pulled up," Kanwer stammered.

"Ok. So let us agree on this. You do not want to grow your hair back again, fine. But, you can't let go of the turban."

"What?" asked Kanwer increduously, not quite believing that he had heard his father correctly.

What on earth is this now, he thought to himself. Kanwer was used to the mind games his father always played with him since his childhood, but this one sounded just too ridiculous.

"From now on, whenever you go out, the turban should be on your head. Do whatever you want to do in the house. But when you go out, you will wear the turban. Am I clear?"

"How does that make any sense, Dad?"

"It does. What will people think? That Brig. Cheema's son has cut his hair? Do you realize how embarrassing this is?"

"Dad, come on. Most of your friends' kids have cut their hair."

"You only have one choice."

"What if I don't agree?"

"Then, I will make sure you do not get a penny from my property after my death. I will donate everything I have to the gurudwara."

Not again, Kanwer thought to himself. His father had used this line so many times in the last few years that by now it just didn't count any more. But, it seemed, the only way to end this deadlock was to accept his condition.

"Ok. Dad. I accept it. I will wear a turban whenever I go out."

No words were exchanged after that. Brig. Cheema just nodded ever so briefly and went to his room.

A smile of relief slowly spread across Mrs. Cheema's face. She wiped her tears and escorted her son to his room. The mother and son spoke till late about how unreasonable his father was. Ah! Mothers!

~

There is a great buzz in the campus today about the five exchange students expected from France. They are going to study at Fergusson College for a month, as part of a student exchange programme between their college and a commerce college from France. Unlike the regular year long programme, they are to be here just for a month long induction project.

Kanwer tries to spot his gang of friends near the parking lot. Not seeing them at their usual hang out, he makes his way towards the college canteen. His heart is thudding loudly, his mind trying to anticipate the reaction of his friends to his turban-less look.

He sees them on one of the tables near the TV area, engrossed in a loud banter, as always. Kanwer walks towards them. Sharad Panicker, his best friend, who is facing him, looks at him with raised eyebrows, while the others turn around to see what has caught his attention. Kanwer is amused to see their reaction though it is exactly as he had imagined it to be.

"What the hell, dude! Is that really you??" Sharad asks not quite believing his eyes.

Kanwer grins widely, running his hand through his short cropped hair while the others react exactly the way Sharad did, loud guffaws punctuated with exclamations.

Kanwer pulls up a vacant chair from the adjacent table and sits down with his gang.

They are still scanning him carefully to confirm that he is the same guy. Another friend, Rohit Shah pulls his hair to confirm it is not a wig!

"Sheesh...guys, lay off now!" says Kanwer, acting like he is annoyed now.

"Not really. But how did Amrish allow you to do this?" enquires Sharad.

Amrish Puri is the gang's nickname for Brig. Cheema - the iconic villain of Bollywood - known for playing a typical strict Indian father in the super hit movie *Dilwale Dulhania Le Jayenge*. Sharad's father is addressed as 'Champu' because of his perennially over-oiled hair while Rohit's father is referred to as 'Gujjubhai' for his thick Gujarati accent.

"Dude, don't even ask about that. Long story. Will tell you later. Tell me something cool. What's with the college kids going gaga about the Fr..."

"Did you see the French chicks?" asks Sharad cutting Kanwer short.

"No man, I just directly came here," replies Kanwar.

"Oh! They are super hot, the girls! There are two boys and three girls," says Rohit getting all pumped up.

"Shhhhh......," the usually quiet Aakash gestures them to keep quiet.

The group sees the exchange students enter the canteen. All eyes are fixed on the new entrants. The French exchange students are clearly both embarrassed and intimidated. But, not Hadoune Karim. Hadoune Karim is the odd one out in the group. She wears a hijab and appears to be a French Muslim. But, she is the most striking of them all. Confident, elegant and, at 5'11", she towers above all.

The French students order some sandwiches and cold drinks, as the others in the canteen continue staring at them unabashedly.

~

Four weeks later

Kanwer is placed in the same group as Hadoune in the accounts group and they become good friends. Kanwer is amazed at the way Hadoune can grasp even the toughest of concepts so easily. She is a very smart girl with a striking personality. Unlike the others in the group, she has a surprisingly good command over English and because of which she is able to get along easily with her new classmates.

Meanwhile, Kanwer had stopped the turban-removing-in-the-bylane drama, after his father spotted him, or rather caught him red-handed putting the turban back on this head, near the entrance gate of the society building in which the Cheema family lived. Of course, there was a huge ruckus in the house which eventually subsided after severals days of a silent, cold war.

It has been three and a half weeks since the arrival of the French students. Preparations for their farewell function have begun. Not surprisingly, Hadoune is selected as the female host of the function. Kanwer sees her sitting on the steps of Kimaya, the open air theatre of Fergusson College.

She is making some notes in Hinglish for her hosting performance the next day.

"Hey Hadoune, what's up?" asks Kanwer as he climbs up the stairs and sits next to her.

"Oh...hi..." Hadoune looks surprised. "All good. I was just thinking about you. Wanted some help for my script. Good you came."

"Ya. Sure. I would love to. Let me know what you need from me."

"I am very hungry. Let's go to Good Luck Cafe and speak about it there."

"Oh ya! Why not! Let me call your friend Marion as well. I met him on my way here and he wanted me to take him along if we were going to Good Luck."

"Fantastic. Let's do that."

Marion, Hadoune and Kanwer enter the Good Luck Cafe, a famous Irani cafe-restaurant located at the FC road junction. It is frequented by the students of all the colleges nearby and is particularly famous for its delicious *bun maska* and tea.

Waiting for their *bun maska* to arrive the trio start chatting.

"Hey Kanwer! I saw pictures of you in...err...on... Facebook. You h...had a turban earlier, eh? Looking very cool!," says Marion in broken English. The mention of his turban, suddenly out of nowhere, takes Kanwer by surprise.

"Oh! Turban! Is it!" Hadoune looks surprised.

Kanwer manages a sheepish grin with an unintelligible word which they assumed was a 'yes'.

"Show me the picture, Marion," says Hadoune, getting all excited

Marion whips out his iphone and shows some of Kanwer's old pictures to her. Kanwer is meanwhile sitting there with a sheepish expression, a mix of embarrassment, awkwardness and confusion.

"Come on guys! Here comes our order. Let's eat and get to work," Kanwer tries to change the topic

"Hey Kanwer, can I ask you something if you don't mind?" says Hadoune

"Ya...sure."

"Why did you stop wearing a turban?"

"No reason in particular...Just like that."

"Ok...But it made you look so distinctive and so...handsome. Were you wearing it for a religious reason?"

"Well...ya...I am a Sikh so it is a part of our identity...We were well...ahem...mmmm...a warrior clan, you can say...Well...actually Sikhs have to keep long hair which then is knotted on the top of the head and wearing the turban is hard work," stammered Kanwer, not quite sure of himself.

"A Sikh! Ok...I will read up on that..Sounds interesting. But why did you cut your hair then?" asks Hadoune as she listens carefully to Kanwer's answer.

"I don't know. I was tired of looking different. I wanted to look like everybody else around me."

"Oh. That's strange! I wear a *hijab* because it is part of my identity too and it does not really affect anything I do or think."

"Don't tell me you were not bullied in school back home in France because of it."

"Well. I was. But then what difference does that make? Of course, I got bullied for wearing a *hijab* and for being a Muslim but I also got bulled for being too tall and skinny and blah..blah...so what?"

"Ok...fine...let's discuss your script now. Then we have the business communication class at four."

"Oh ya...cool...As you say," replies Hadoune taking out her hosting script.

~

The next day, Hadoune spots Kanwer in the parking lot and runs up to him.

"Hey Kanwer!"

"Oh hi! What's up?"

"You came early today?" she asks

"Yo, man...was getting bored at home so thought I will hang out here with my friends."

"That's cool," says Hadoune. She is unusually mellow today.

"Kanwer, I was up late till last night reading up on Sikhism."

"Hey Hadoune, if you don't mind, I gotta go..." interrupts Kanwer.

Hadoune stood watching as he sped off on his bike. She assumed he got offended at the topic of cutting his hair which she had been bringing up. Deep inside, she feels a deep sense of regret for having done that in the first place.

The farewell function was to be held that evening and it was their last day in the campus.

~

Eight years later

Picnickers from nearby Chandigarh are enjoying the cool evening breeze at the popular Vista Point at Bhakra Nangal Dam, when suddenly the air is rent with loud screams and shouts.

"Help...help...helppppp."

A strong current of water has washed away two girls from where they were standing along with their friends at the bank of the river, and now they are flailing and floundering in the water. A large crowd of people has gathered there but they are just looking on helplessly, while a couple of them are trying to call the authorities.

The girls don't look like they are more than twelve or thirteen years old. Their friends, of the same age as them, are crying and running helter-skelter. They have no clue what to do. They have come from the nearby Naina Devi town, bunking their day school.

Some alert onlookers see a wire lying on the ground and throw it towards the girls. One of the girls manages to catch it, but, just then the wire snaps.

The girls are barely able to keep their heads above the water and the onlookers are losing hope of saving the girls.

"Help...helpppppppppppp"

Suddenly, somebody hurls a rope towards the girls.

It is not a rope. It is a long piece of cloth.

It has a medium-sized stone tied on the end that is thrown in the water while the other end is tied to a Maruti Gypsy.

The girls desperately cling on to the piece of cloth. The baffled crowd looks to see where this 'cloth rope' is coming from. And from behind the Gypsy emerges a young Sikh army officer.

Captain Kanwer Singh Cheema.

The piece of cloth that he has thrown into the water to save the girls is his turban.

Blood in the Ballot Box

I am Dalbir Singh, the only son of Punjab's Chief Minister and this is my story.

I was born in 1975 at Nanaksar Jaito village in Faridkot district of Punjab, to the then Faridkot MP Gurdarshan Singh and Baljeet Kaur, a housewife. They say I was born with a silver spoon in my mouth. I don't understand what the big deal in that is. Yes, my family is very wealthy and influential in this part of the country. But, a lot of people are born into privileged families, I am not the only one. Wonder why am I always reminded of it, every single day of my twenty six years of existence.

But, nevertheless let me continue my story.

Needless to say, for my family, I was the apple of their eye. I did my schooling from the Doon School, Dehradun. Ah! Those were the days! My gang and I had great fun and I can vividly recall each and every memory of school. I am still in touch with most of my friends, Aman Kapoor, son of the famous filmmaker Ranjan

Kapoor; Ayaan and Vivaan Singhania, twin sons of India's leading industrialist Rajendra Singhania, and Emaan Yadav, son of the sugar baron of Uttar Pradesh, Lal Yadav.

After passing out from school, I was sent to the hallowed London School of Economics to pursue higher studies.

Every year that I was in London, I would return to Punjab, once during the summer vacation and then again during the Christmas break. My air tickets would always reach me a week before I was to depart. By the time I was twenty-two, my father had become the chief minister of Punjab. And oh, let me talk about the most important bit here, the kind of security I would get back home made me feel like a king. It was quite incredible to be treated that way. Excuse me for sounding arrogant but, let me tell you, nobody, but the ones who have received this kind of treatment know how it feels.

By then, my family had shifted to Chandigarh, the capital of Punjab. My father informally started including me in most of his important meetings. I had always found politics very interesting, and in Punjab it was like a 'war' every single day. My father's party, the Punjab Janta Party (PJP) had won that year's state election again, with a resounding majority. I have always been very proud of my father and it was evident that the people loved him too.

I can still recall the awestruck faces of my friends in London when I would show them the pictures of my father's political rallies. Hundreds and thousands of people, as far as one's eyes could see. In his thirty years of political career, my father had acquired considerable administrative experience and shrewd political skills and boasted of a large loyal following.

It was around then time that for the first time in my life I accompanied by father to a political rally. This was just a thank-you-for-your-support kind of a rally, not one of those high-on-tension rallies that are held before elections.

I arrived with my father in a large entourage of twenty white Ambassador cars, the vehicle of choice of politicians in those days. The security arrangements were unprecedented. On my way, I could see that the rally was causing inconvenience to the local commuters with even ambulances stuck and traffic being re-routed to allow us VVIPs to make it to the venue of the rally without a hassle. But it did not quite matter, I felt. People like my father who get this treatment deserve it, as they work hard for it. Being a politician is just another profession, albeit with more perks than other jobs. Being a part of this, it was easy to understand why power is more important than money and why politicians are treated more deferentially than even the most successful businessmen in the social hierarchy of Punjab.

We reached the venue and as expected, it was a setting typical of such rallies in India. A huge open ground, blaring loudspeakers, dust all over the place and a well decorated makeshift stage made from wooden planks which are infamous for breaking down, resulting in hilarious scenes with politicians and their side-kicks falling over each other.

A large number of supporters had turned up for the rally, held in a village called Zirakpur near Chandigarh. There were an estimated ten thousand people at the rally holding hand painted banners, as they chanted *'CM Sahab Zindabad'*. Ten chairs were placed on the stage, on which the crème de la crème of the party was to sit. I looked around and noticed that six of the chairs were to be occupied by our relatives, who were all part of my father's cabinet.

My father was made to sit on the biggest chair in the middle and I sat on a smaller chair next to him. His chair was a bigger version of the one used to seat the bride and the groom on their wedding reception day. A big red chair with a golden border.

As my father took the podium, the crowd erupted in joy. My father was a man of few words but a great showman. He was a good orator though an occasional one. He enthralled the supporters with a great speech and expansive hand gestures. His promises seemed genuine and his grand plans sounded achievable, so much so that by the time his speech ended I could feel goosebumps.

When we got back home, I remember asking him matter-of-factly, "Papa ji, so do you really have grand plans to change Punjab, especially the infrastructure?"

Ah! How naive and idealistic I was!

My father just twirled his moustache and smiled. He knew I required a great deal of political exposure and training, quite contrary to what I thought about myself at that time.

"Papa ji...am serious...and frankly, especially the cities are quite an embarrassment. Remember, when my English friends came down two years ago, how appalled they were when we took them to Amritsar....surely the urban infrastructure can easily be fixed...?"

"Haha...let's hope so, sonny. In Punjab politics, considerable part of the ruling party's energies are consumed in keeping the numerous opponents at bay."

"Oh! Come on Papa ji!...That can't consume all of your time."

He let out a thunderous laugh. Other than being an astute politician, he was a very dynamic businessman who had grown the family business manifold in the last twenty years.

"My dear son, administrators in England do not have to deal with the stuff we deal with here. The whole caste dynamics, the religion angle, the ongoing ego clash with the central government and so many other issues..."

"Come on, Papa ji, I am sure they must be having their own problems in England, yet development happens. We see progress there every day. Here in Punjab, it seems we are going backwards."

"Well, here it is impossible to separate politics from religion and caste and that is what takes up most of my energy. You will realize once you join me."

I thought my father was being too sceptic.

I left for London soon after to complete my studies.

~

Four years after my father became the Punjab CM, I returned to Punjab to join politics full time.

Nothing had changed in the last four years. Absolutely nothing.

Though it was a big transition from the organised and modern London to chaotic Punjab, deep inside, I was happy. Ever since I could remember, I knew I wanted to be in politics and had been preparing for it.

Elections were approaching again the next year. The political situation was extremely tense this time. My father's sister-in-law, Gurdayal Kaur, who was the finance minister in his cabinet, was planning go to her separate way. The reason was my father's refusal to elevate her inexperienced son, Parvinder Singh, to a cabinet rank. She was rumoured to be starting her own party, but that was no cause for worry as she was not a very popular figure in the state politics and couldn't hold on her own under any circumstances.

My father was right in not agreeing to my aunt's request because Parvinder not only was inexperienced but was a huge embarrassment for my father's party. The year before, he had kidnapped, raped and killed a girl, after she rejected his marriage proposal. The daughter of a small time shop owner, she was abducted by Parvinder and his accomplices in broad daylight from a popular market area. What a fool!

My father too had often broken the law, but not like this. In Punjab, if you want to be seen as powerful, you need to know how to bend the law, but you should be smart enough to do it in the 'right' way without getting caught.

Ok. Ok. Before you judge me for justifying such things, let me invite you to Punjab. Live our life to know that there is no other way. This is the only way.

Parvinder's men had threatened and intimidated the girl's father so that he did not testify against him. Parvinder got off scot-free despite tremendous pressure from national womens' groups.

Parvinder's father, my uncle, was rumoured to be a 'crazy' man. He had witnessed my father kill a business accomplice, who was caught cheating in our family garment export business. My uncle threatened to call the police and expose my father. In the heat of the moment, my aunt who was present at the scene, shot my uncle with his own pistol. The next morning the murder was declared a 'suicide'. Eternally grateful, from then on my father was always very accomodating towards my aunt, and she made sure that he never ever forgot that he owed his life to her.

Born into a middle class family of teachers, my aunt was an extremely ambitious woman, willing to go to any lengths to get what she wanted. She was extremely fond of expensive jewellery and designer silk suits and her wardrobe could give any top film actress a run for her money. My aunt was a widow, which meant that she was not to be seen in public wearing fancy and colourful clothes. Her transformation at public rallies and functions was surprising where she would wear simple, pastel coloured cotton clothes with her head demurely covered with a dupatta.

≈

The memories of that day are still fresh in my mind. It was a

Sunday. My father, mother and I were watching TV in the drawing room. My aunt was on TV speaking to a leading journalist on a popular news channel. She had joined our long time rival political party, Bharat Unionist Party (BUP), which had a significant national presence unlike our party, which was a dominant force only in Punjab. BUP had not been doing too well in Punjab and their state head, Ramlal Garg, was desperate to win this time.

In between the interview, the channel was showing shots of my aunt's induction ceremony into BUP. She had a big smile on her face as if she had already won the election with a huge margin.

'The PJP is not in a mood to introspect, and their total failure on all fronts in fulfilling their election promises is being covered up by crimes such as maiming and killing political opponents. We will be making some really sensational revelations in the days to come, which will obliterate Gurdarshan Singh and his party from the face of this earth,' thundered Gurdayal Kaur in a menacing tone.

Sensational revelations!!

What the hell did she mean by that?

I looked at my father to see his reaction. He was seething with anger but he was also looking scared. I had never ever seen him like this in my life. He always wore the same expression, no matter what was happening around him. After all he was used to dirty politics and all that which comes with it.

Abruptly he got up and left. I was about to go after him to understand what made him so angry, when my mother gestured to me to keep sitting. She murmured under her breath that it was wise not to bombard him with questions at this point. Obviously, she knew something I did not. Unbeknownst to all, my mother was a passive participant in my father's political life. To a layman, it would appear that she was completely out of sync with the happenings around her, but the truth was the exact opposite. She had been a strong but an invisible and silent supporter of my father all through his life.

The opposition was accusing my father of amassing wealth disproportionate to his business income and of using his political clout to further his business interests, an accusation which he aggressively denied on all public platforms. But I knew this was true. Out of several such instances, I was aware of this one, when he had used his influence and power to allot government land to his own garment export firm and I was made to sign various documents for it. I strongly believe that if we are working so hard to benefit the people, we also have the right to use some power for our benefit.

Adding to our woes was the fact that my father's party which had ruled the State for the last fourteen years, was struggling to retain its political and religious supremacy. In the midst of the agrarian crisis, anti-incumbency and allegations of corruption, the party's attempts to retain its core Sikh votes were backfiring. Meanwhile, the BUP, which till now was struggling to make some dent, saw the situation as a God sent opportunity and wasted no time against the supposed 'misrule'.

Later in the evening, my father called for a meeting with his close group of party members, the only people he trusted. One of those was my *mama*, my mother's brother, Amrit Singh. He was my father's go-to man for anything that needed to be done. Intimidating, bullying, threatening and even beating up people were his core competencies.

In the meeting my *mama* revealed that my aunt was planning to release a clip to the media, which had my father and him talking about killing a policeman, who was known to be close to Ramlal Garg. For three long hours there was instense deliberation and brain storming about the best way to counter this assault. By the end of the meeting, we had chalked out our strategy to silence our detractors.

The next morning, pictures of the father of the girl who was raped and killed by Parvinder, were all over the newspapers. Backed by us, the girl's father was ready to re-open the case against Parvinder.

Gotcha this time, dear aunty...!

The next morning, I was sitting in the garden with my father, sipping tea, when the phone rang. My father who seemed to be expecting this call smirked and instructed the servant to get the cordless phone receiver to him, in the garden itself.

My father put the call on loudspeaker mode.

"Sat Sri Akal Bhai sahib ji," said a familiar voice curtly from the other end of the phone.

No prizes for guessing who it was. My poor scared aunt, of course.

"Sat Sri Akalji, Who is this? Hmmmm...Let me guess..." Papa ji said in a sarcastic tone, knowing very well who the person on the other side was.

'What can we do to fix this?' she asked, without attempting to answer his question.

"Fix what?"

"You know what?"

"Well, if you are indeed that smart, then you know what we want."

I smiled, as my father twirled his moustache. The code language they used was very filmy but by now I was no newcomer to these kinds of conversations.

"Let's say, I will give you what you want and I want this matter closed for good then."

"Let's call it a deal. I will wait for your message."

"Ok." She slammed the phone down, making her anger evident.

Within an hour of that call, my *mama* Amrit Singh received a sealed envelope. Inside the envelope was a sheet of paper with an Old Delhi address, the next day's date and a time printed on it and at the bottom of the page was written; Parvinder, Albel, Amrit and Dalbir.

Parvinder and I were supposed to meet up at the Delhi address in the presence of Amrit Singh and Albel Singh. Albel Singh was my aunt's right hand man. She was widely rumoured to be having an illicit relationship with him.

The next morning, my *mama* and I, along with our driver Subhash left for Delhi, for our rendevous. We knew we would be watched and had decided that the remaining security would join us at Ambala, as there was nothing to fear as long as we were in Punjab.

A six member security team led by Satish Hooda joined us in two civilian cars from the village Sadopur, a few kilometres before Ambala city. Satish Hooda or Hoodaji, as I fondly called him was a retired army man and my father's security advisor. We stopped at a highway restaurant near Shahbaad Markanda for breakfast. While Subhash waited for us in the car, Hoodaji and two of his security men followed us inside.

After finishing our breakfast, we came out of the restaurant and saw Subhash paying a *chai-wallah*. The *chai-wallah* left as we approached the car.

Subhash opened the door of the car for me to get in, but Hoodaji suddenly grabbed my arm and pulled me away, "Get into my car," he whispered in my ear.

I was a little taken aback but sat in his car along with my *mama* and Hoodaji in the back seat.

No sooner did Hoodaji's car pull out from the restaurant's parking lot on to the highway, we heard a loud explosion. Our car came to a screeching halt.

We looked back to see the car I was supposed to be in, going up in flames.

"Get that *chai-wallah*...," shouted an enraged Hoodaji as the heavily built man sitting in the front seat of our car sprinted towards the restaurant.

I sat there stunned, disoriented and seething with anger.

Damn you, aunty! It doesn't end here, you wretched woman.

Son of a Cabbie

Jorawar Singh, a classic case of an ABCD, had been living two lives at a time. For the uninitiated, ABCD is the widely referred to abbreviation of American Born Confused Desi. He is also, what they call in New York, the 'son of an archetypal cabbie'.

~

Jorawar Singh's father Lakhan Singh, a garrulous but hard working village simpleton, is a cab driver who migrated from his native village Nainowal Jattan in Punjab, back in the early 1980s. There was a large wave of immigration after the 1984 Sikh riots in New Delhi when a large number of Sikhs like Lakhan Singh fearing for their safety in India left their villages in Punjab for foreign shores.

Lakhan Singh had earlier planned to go to Calcutta as all his relatives from his mother's side were working there at that time. He was enamoured with the Calcutta way of life, after seeing pictures of his relatives posing in front of Victoria Memorial and riding in trams. But, after the 1984 happenings, he left for America instead, the promised land of hope and opportunity.

For the first three years in New York, he struggled to make ends meet by doing odd jobs; the most noteworthy of them being that of a car cleaner. He stayed in a ghetto and worked for long hours without saving much. Seeing Lakhan Singh's plight, his sixty year old Indian well-wisher and neighbour, Randhir Singh told him that his value in the marriage market back in Punjab would be less as compared to others, as he had no money and advised him to somehow get a cab license.

After another five years of great hardship and struggle, Lakhan, managed to save some money to get a license and also buy a cab. It was the happiest moment of his life.

Eight years later Lakhan Singh went back to his village to get a bride for himself. In those days, even the village *zamindaar* would go out on a limb to marry his only daughter to a man who had lived or even travelled abroad once. It did not matter, what he did or who he was. Lakhan was happy as could be when he realized that he was the most sought after boy in his village. His mother, Bachan Kaur, had already done the groundwork and shortlisted five potential brides from nearby villages.

After a very careful evaluation, Lakhan culled out the best 'candidate' using the black and white studio-clicked pictures of the prospective brides. All the photos had a similar background, which made him wonder whether all the girls were from the same family or stayed next door to the same photo studio. Like all other young men in Punjab in those times, Lakhan too was looking for a girl who was traditional and docile. He was happy with the choice of his prospective bride, who appeared to be the meekest of the lot.

But, as luck would have it, before Bachan Kaur could manage to speak to the parents of the chosen girl, she got the news that the girl had run away with an old paramour of hers.

"*Bebe*, I don't want to get married. What if the others run away as well?" a dejected Lakhan asked his mother this innocent question.

"Don't be a fool," Bachan Kaur responded sharply.

"What if the girl runs away when I take here to *Amreeke*? What if somebody is waiting for her there?"

"Hold your tongue and choose another girl from the photos I gave you, you bird-brained boy."

Dejected and heart broken, Lakhan randomly picked up a photo, and married the girl featured in that photo.

On his wedding night, his paternal uncle, Kirpal Singh, gave him opium, as was usually the norm in their village. This fact was repeatedly highlighted to his friends by Lakhan in the years to come, followed by peals of laughter.

A week after his wedding Lakhan Singh left for New York and precisely nine months later, Jorawar was born. When Jorawar was a year old, Lakhan took his wife and son to New York. Nine months after setting foot in New York, Jorawar's sister, Manpreet was born.

~

Eighteen years have passed since, but even today, Lakhan Singh is a man who can talk till the cows come home and can work his fingers to the bone. His son, Jorawar, a 6'1" tall, *patka* (a head covering worn by young Sikh boys) wearing boy, avoided his father like the plague, as he would go on and on with his anecdotes that would make even the most experienced raconteur fade in comparison.

An excerpt from a typical conversation his father would have with his friends over drinks occasionally or rather, a typical monologue his father would give to his friends over drinks every weekend: his father would be the one talking most of the time. As the night progressed, his voice would grow louder while the jokes became lamer.

"Goldie, let me tell you a joke. When one get married, the man taalks and the *vooman* listens, *aphter* a *phew* years, the *vooman taalks* and the man listens, *aphter* the childrens grow up, both *taalks* and the neighbours listen...hahahahah...but but...seriously...I...I am telling ju...our *voomen hab ther brainz in thr kneez.* Lookkk at *thez goris.* They *rilly* smart, but *bunn* thing I hate about them *iz thish* whole smoking and drinking part. Am telling *ju*...only in this matter, our *voomen* are better *butt een eberything* else, they are much better...these *vite vite goriz*... Oh ya, how can I forget the *goriz* are characterless too...theze *goris*...bloody...keep your *sonz avay fram* these *goriz*...n those black *girlz* as well...they do drugs...aal the damn time..this country is going to the *dawgs*..am tellin *ju*.."

To add to his woes, Jorawar's mother always had a bone to pick with his father. She was always ready to blow her top at the drop of a hat. She was far from being a docile girl, that his father and grandmother had so wished for.

It was a non-stop *Mahabharata* in their madcap house all the time and Jorawar was Yudhisthira. His grandmother, who lived with them after her husband's death, was the Shakuni of the house, and would leave no chance to add fuel to the fire. (*Mahabharata* is an ancient Indian epic and is widely described as 'the longest poem ever written'. The core story is that of a dynastic struggle for the throne of Hastinapura, an ancient kingdom which eventually culminates in the great but exceedingly long battle of Kurukhshetra. Yudhisthira was the rightful heir to the throne of Hastinapura and was known to be an ethical and a righteous chap who was considered a victim of the circumstances around him.)

Outside the house, Jorawar's life was like that of any other brown immigrant teenager in the Richmond Hill area of the borough of Queens. His family lived comfortably and faced the usual challenges, including the most obvious one, racism, outside their Sikh dominated area. Like all other children of Punjabi immigrants, Jorawar too was always trying to forge a distinctive identity in which he was required to balance the time-honoured ideals of his parent's heritage with the individualistic oriented lifestyle of urban America.

It saddened Jorawar to see that his family was no better than a typical broken American family, that was so looked down upon in his Sikh community. Add to that, the societal pressure of acting a certain way to ensure that he came across as a respectful conventional Sikh boy. He also lamented the fact that his parents, especially his father treated him and his sister differently. There were double standards when it came to raising a girl vis-à-vis bringing up a boy. The girls were supposed to be submissive and mostly engage in domestic tasks. They had to know how to cook Punjabi food and to wear their dupattas right.

Sample this discussion between his mother, Rani and their neighbourhood aunty Mrs. Thind, which took place last week.

Rani : Did you see the suit Sheenu's daughter wore to the gurudwara yesterday?

Mrs. Thind : Yes. Total *Fitteh mooh*....it was so bad...(*Fitteh mooh*, is the Punjabi version of facepalm which means smiting one's face in exasperation.)

Rani : She is nineteen, but doesn't even know how to drape the dupatta properly over her head.

Mrs. Thind : Tch...Tch...What *jaloos*! (*Jaloos* is the Punjabi way of referring to someone as a total mess.)

Rani : By the way, don't tell this to anyone but I think I saw her with a *gora* (white skinned) last month. They were walking hand in hand in the forest park. Please don't tell anyone, ok? Otherwise, they will blame me for maligning their daughter's reputation, which is, in any case, non-existent.

Mrs. Thind : No...No...Don't worry...I won't. I will take this secret to my grave. But what a shameless thing to do! Know what! I always had a feeling this girl would do something like this. I feel bad for her parents.

Rani : What bad? I blame her upbringing for that. Look at my daughter, Mani. She is also born and brought up here, but she can never ever do such a thing. I can vouch for that.

Mrs. Thind : Yes. I agree. *Chalo* I will make a move. We have to go to Brooklyn today to see a boy for my brother's daughter.

Rani : For whom? Sandeep?

Mrs. Thind : Uh...no...For the older one, Gurdeep. Will see you later.

Rani : But she got engaged just two months ago...All well?

Mrs. Thind : The wedding was called off...See you tom...

Rani : From your side or their's?

Mrs. Thind : Uhh...mm...Our side. We came to know that the boy was a d...drug addict. Ok. Then. Bye...Getting late...

Rani : Ok. Sad to hear that. I had told you earlier only not to go for these kinds of boys from the advertisement field. Only doctors and engineers are safe bets. Anyway, give my regards to your brother. Tell him, with God's grace, he will find a good boy for Gurdeep. Just be careful this time...And let me know if you need my help in checking his background or anything. I know half of Brooklyn. Ok?

Mrs. Thind : Yes. Yes, of course. *Sat Sri Akal, Bhainji.*

The moment Mrs. Thind left, Rani picked up the phone and called all her other friends and told them about Mrs. Thind's brother's daughter's broken engagement. All conversations started and ended with, 'Don't tell anybody, ok?'

~

Jorawar didn't entirely blame his mother for the person she had become. She had suffered all her life and as a child, Jorawar had often witnessed his mother getting beaten up by his father. The reasons ranged from, 'Why have you put so much salt in the food?' to 'I think you are having an affair with Gurnaam Singh!' Now, as the parents are getting old the situation is the exact opposite. His father faces the brunt of his irate mother all the time.

Jorawar reckoned that his mother was the happiest when she went to Punjab to meet her parents and extended family once every year. Jorawar and Manpreet would accompany their mother on this annual visit. She loved blowing her own trumpet about her life back in New York in front of her relatives, especially her sisters Satti and Jindo.

Jorawar's mother was very competitive towards both her sisters, though outwardly, they were thick as thieves and she would speak to them on the phone every other day. They always tried to be one up against the other in all matters, ranging from their kids' heights to who has better clothes. The sisters, Satti and Jindo, held a grudge against Rani for not helping them migrate to America, as is usually expected by the relatives of the person who goes abroad.

Satti now lived with her parents, after she had fallen victim to a fraud NRI marriage. In spite of this personal misfortune, Satti went on to do a basic General Nursing and Midwifery course and got a decent job for herself in a government hospital. She was the only one among her sisters who was working. Jindo, being the prettier one (after Rani, of course who was the prettiest and landed an NRI for herself) was married off to a rich landlord family in the neighbouring village. She had done a teacher's course and was a teacher before her marriage, but was not allowed to work after marriage. She kept herself busy in taking care of her five children; four girls and a boy. The boy was the youngest, after the first four pregnancies brought forth girls into the world. After the birth of the boy, Jindo bore no more children.

A typical conversation amongst the three sisters, when Rani went visiting them in Punjab, would go something like this.

Rani : *Chi...chi*...India is full of flies and mosquitoes. You will not find a single fly at our place.

Satti : Really?

Rani : Yes. Yes. Why would I lie? I would not set foot in this country, if you two were not here.

Jindo : Huh! Then you should have called us there.

Rani : Again the same topic! If I could have, I would have called you there. But the rules became stringent. What could I have done?

This topic was always followed by bouts of sullen silence.

Satti : How is Manpreet? She didn't come this time?

Rani : She is fine. She has her exams next month, so couldn't come.

Jorawar knew the real reason his sister had not accompanied him and his mother to India this time. Manpreet was a typical ABCD girl when it came to her dressing style or the movies she watched. She had huge Bollywood aspirations, like most of her friends, who had grown up watching Shahrukh Khan movies. Manpreet was convinced that one day, she would find a guy who would sing and serenade her in a sunflower-filled field. The real reason for her not coming to India was that a Bollywood movie was being shot in her college campus and she did not want to miss it.

Satti : She could have got her books and studied here.

Rani : In this biting cold weather? Yeah, right!

Jindo : I think you forget that it is colder there, Rani.

Rani : Yeah. But we have heating in our houses there. Not like India, where one almost dies of cold.

Jindo : Ok...Ok...Fine. We are all dying here every year, that's right. Anyway, are you searching for a suitable girl for Jorawar?

Rani : We don't live in India that we have to marry off our kids at this age. In America, kids get married only after twenty-five.

Jindo : Oh my god! That's so late. When will they have kids then? Thank heavens, we did not go there. Anyway, I have heard that boys there are marrying boys. Tch...tch...tch...

Rani : No...No...Nothing like that. All hearsay! What do people here know about America? They waste their entire day running after cows and buffaloes.

Satti : Rani, now don't say there are no cows or buffaloes there.... hahahhahaha..

By now, Jorawar had gotten used to such comments that were replete with sarcasm and taunts.

All his life, he had felt like he was caught between two worlds that had nothing in common with each other. He was in a constant dilemma as he felt he did not belong to either of these worlds. He had borne the brunt of being a brown guy in a white man's land all his life. And then on his visits back 'home', it was evident that this was not a place he identified with either, even though everybody here looked like him. Growing up, he had heard people call him a coconut, terrorist, browny, bin laden, son of a cabbie, paki. Getting un-boarded from planes, refused internships and being bullied in school were a part of his life and it had become worse after the 9/11 terrorist attack.

He can, even today, vividly recall that day. His father had came back home earlier than usual and looked like he had seen a ghost. Manpreet and he were locked in a room, as the parents huddled in front of the TV, like everybody else in America that day. The next day, he could figure out what had happened but that did not explain why they should be scared. He remembers this conversation he had with his father, when he was eleven years old, in the aftermath of the 9/11 episode.

Jorawar : *Bapuji*, why are we scared? We didn't do anything wrong, did we?

Lakhan Singh : No.

Jorawar : Then?

Lakhan Singh : What then?

Jorawar : Then, why are we not going to school since a week?

Lakhan Singh : Shut up and go to your room!

This was how the repercussions of 9/11 were explained to Jorawar. It was only when he did his own fact-finding that he understood why it would affect his life from thereon.

~

It is a cold November day in 2011. Jorawar is standing in the middle of a chaotic street. He had arrived in Punjab earlier this month with his family for their annual fifteen day visit.

Jorawar looks around to see people and shops crammed into the smallest of spaces and the streets bustling with visitors. The narrow alleys are thronging with hawkers, rickshaws and cows. He can see a mass of colour all around him. He feels as if every sense in his body has suddenly come alive with the noise, sights and scents. People, bikes, mopeds, cars, rickshaws and carts and animals seem to be coming straight him from every angle as he winds through the narrow snake-like alleys.

Last night, without telling anyone, Jorawar took a train from

Hoshiarpur railway station to Amritsar. According to the photographs in their family albums, apparently, he has been to Amritsar twice before as a kid, but Jorawar has no memories of it.

He feels at peace as he walks towards the Golden Temple complex amidst the confusion and chaos around him. He deposits his shoes at a very professional looking shoe storage facility. He is smiling to himself as he climbs up the crowded stairs after washing his feet.

The last year had been particularly stressful for him and he is at a stage in his life where he is desperately looking for some answers.

There are people all around him. As he climbs up the last step of the marble staircase, he sees the Golden Temple for the first time. It is the most majestic thing he has seen in his life and its beauty and serenity takes his breath away. He could never imagine that such a sight could exist amidst such chaos.

The Golden Temple is squeaky clean in contrast to the filthy narrow lanes outside; the complex is breathtakingly stunning with thousands of devotees walking towards the main gurudwara building.

Jorawar can hear the *gurbani* from inside the gurudwara.

"Gur mili-ai ham ka-o sareer sudh bha-ee. (Meeting the Guru, I came to understand my body.)

"Ha-umai tarisnaa sabh agan bujh-ee." (The fires of ego and desire have been totally quenched.)

He walks towards the Temple, as he listens to each and every word of the *gurbani* being spoken.

"Binsay krodh khimaa geh la-ee." (Anger has been dispelled, and I have grasped hold of tolerance.)

He turns to look back towards the entrance from where he had entered. A slight smile crosses his face.

He is free.

He is at peace.

He forgives his father.

He forgives everybody who has bullied him.

He has found what he was looking for.

He has found home.

●●●

Rajpal & Sons was established in 1912 at Lahore. In the early days books on spirituality, social and political issues, and of patriotic nature were published in Hindi, Urdu, English and Punjabi.

In 1947 Rajpal & Sons shifted to Delhi where it soon came to be recognized as India's leading Hindi literary publisher. Its author list included Ramdhari Singh Dinkar, Mahadevi Verma, Harivanshrai Bachchan, Amritlal Nagar, Shivani, Acharya Chatursen, Vishnu Prabhakar, Rajendra Yadav, Mohan Rakesh, Rangey Raghav and Kamleshwar amongst others. Many of the books published by Rajpal & Sons such as *Madhushala, Kurukshetra, Manas ka Hans, Awaara Masiha, Kitney Pakistan, Ashad ka ek Din* are considered classics in Hindi literature and continue to be popular with successive generations of readers.

Today, Rajpal & Sons publishes in English and Hindi. It has the unique honour of publishing books written by several Indian Presidents and Prime Ministers, foremost among them being Dr APJ Abdul Kalam, and also the Hindi translations of all major books written by the Nobel laureate economist Dr Amartya Sen. Rajpal & Sons has published a series of dictionaries edited by the famous lexicographer Dr Hardev Bahri and hundreds of books for children.

Committed to providing healthy entertainment and knowledge to readers through its books, Rajpal & Sons publishes books in Hindi and English. These books are available at all leading book stores across the country and throughout the world.

Rajpal & Sons

1590, Madarsa Road, Kashmere Gate, Delhi-6 Phone: 011-23869812, 23865483
email: sales@rajpalpublishing.com, facebook: facebook.com/rajpalandsons
website: www.rajpalpublishing.com